# A ROSE IN JEOPARDY

Rosella now felt utterly alone and yet she suddenly found herself whispering,

"Help me, please, please. Help me!"

She thought longingly of Aunt Beatrice. She had missed her terribly, but never so much as at this moment.

And for the first time in a long while, she missed her Mama and her Papa, whom she had so few memories of, only their loving voices and the embrace of their arms.

She clung onto herself desperately.

If only there was someone in the world to hold her, to care for her and speak gentle kind words –

Suddenly she felt that someone was watching her, and she looked up to see the portrait of the young man in the turban hanging on the wall above her.

"Why are you smiling?" she asked him. "Look at me. I am in such despair!"

Her tears welled up in her eyes once again, but then she realised that his smile was not mocking but bold and happy.

His bright dark eyes seemed to be comforting and encouraging her.

"*I* care for you – " he was almost saying.

# THE BARBARA CARTLAND PINK COLLECTION

## Titles in this series

1. The Cross Of Love
2. Love In The Highlands
3. Love Finds The Way
4. The Castle Of Love
5. Love Is Triumphant
6. Stars In The Sky
7. The Ship Of Love
8. A Dangerous Disguise
9. Love Became Theirs
10. Love Drives In
11. Sailing To Love
12. The Star Of Love
13. Music Is The Soul Of Love
14. Love In The East
15. Theirs To Eternity
16. A Paradise On Earth
17. Love Wins In Berlin
18. In Search Of Love
19. Love Rescues Rosanna
20. A Heart In Heaven
21. The House Of Happiness
22. Royalty Defeated By Love
23. The White Witch
24. They Sought Love
25. Love Is The Reason For Living
26. They Found Their Way To Heaven
27. Learning To Love
28. Journey To Happiness
29. A Kiss In The Desert
30. The Heart Of Love
31. The Richness Of Love
32. For Ever And Ever
33. An Unexpected Love
34. Saved By An Angel
35. Touching The Stars
36. Seeking Love
37. Journey To Love
38. The Importance Of Love
39. Love By The Lake
40. A Dream Come True
41. The King Without A Heart
42. The Waters Of Love
43. Danger To The Duke
44. A Perfect Way To Heaven
45. Follow Your Heart
46. In Hiding
47. Rivals For Love
48. A Kiss From The Heart
49. Lovers In London
50. This Way To Heaven
51. A Princess Prays
52. Mine For Ever
53. The Earl's Revenge
54. Love At The Tower
55. Ruled By Love
56. Love Came From Heaven
57. Love And Apollo
58. The Keys Of Love
59. A Castle Of Dreams
60. A Battle Of Brains
61. A Change Of Hearts
62. It Is Love
63. The Triumph Of Love
64. Wanted – A Royal Wife
65. A Kiss Of Love
66. To Heaven With Love
67. Pray For Love
68. The Marquis Is Trapped
69. Hide And Seek For Love
70. Hiding From Love
71. A Teacher Of Love
72. Money Or Love
73. The Revelation Is Love
74. The Tree Of Love
75. The Magnificent Marquis
76. The Castle
77. The Gates Of Paradise
78. A Lucky Star
79. A Heaven On Earth
80. The Healing Hand
81. A Virgin Bride
82. The Trail To Love
83. A Royal Love Match
84. A Steeplechase For Love
85. Love At Last
86. Search For A Wife
87. Secret Love
88. A Miracle Of Love
89. Love And The Clans
90. A Shooting Star
91. The Winning Post Is Love
92. They Touched Heaven
93. The Mountain Of Love
94. The Queen Wins
95. Love And The Gods
96. Joined By Love
97. The Duke Is Deceived
98. A Prayer For Love
99. Love Conquers War
100. A Rose In Jeopardy

# A ROSE IN JEOPARDY

# BARBARA CARTLAND

Barbaracartland.com Ltd

# THE BARBARA CARTLAND PINK COLLECTION

Dame Barbara Cartland is still regarded as the most prolific bestselling author in the history of the world.

In her lifetime she was frequently in the Guinness Book of Records for writing more books than any other living author.

Her most amazing literary feat was to double her output from 10 books a year to over 20 books a year when she was 77 to meet the huge demand.

She went on writing continuously at this rate for 20 years and wrote her very last book at the age of 97, thus completing an incredible 400 books between the ages of 77 and 97.

Her publishers finally could not keep up with this phenomenal output, so at her death in 2000 she left behind an amazing 160 unpublished manuscripts, something that no other author has ever achieved.

Barbara's son, Ian McCorquodale, together with his daughter Iona, felt that it was their sacred duty to publish all these titles for Barbara's millions of admirers all over the world who so love her wonderful romances.

So in 2004 they started publishing the 160 brand new Barbara Cartlands as *The Barbara Cartland Pink Collection*, as Barbara's favourite colour was always pink – and yet more pink!

The Barbara Cartland Pink Collection is published monthly exclusively by Barbaracartland.com and the books are numbered in sequence from 1 to 160.

Enjoy receiving a brand new Barbara Cartland book each month by taking out an annual subscription to the Pink Collection, or purchase the books individually.

The Pink Collection is available from the Barbara Cartland website www.barbaracartland.com via mail order and through all good bookshops.

In addition Ian and Iona are proud to announce that The Barbara Cartland Pink Collection is now available in ebook format as from Valentine's Day 2011.

For more information, please contact us at:

Barbaracartland.com Ltd.
Camfield Place
Hatfield
Hertfordshire AL9 6JE
United Kingdom

Telephone:  +44 (0)1707 642629
Fax:  +44 (0)1707 663041
Email: info@barbaracartland.com

# THE LATE DAME BARBARA CARTLAND

Barbara Cartland who sadly died in May 2000 at the age of nearly 99 was the world's most famous romantic novelist who wrote 723 books in her lifetime with worldwide sales of over 1 billion copies and her books were translated into 36 different languages.

As well as romantic novels, she wrote historical biographies, 6 autobiographies, theatrical plays, books of advice on life, love, vitamins and cookery. She also found time to be a political speaker and television and radio personality.

She wrote her first book at the age of 21 and this was called *Jigsaw*. It became an immediate bestseller and sold 100,000 copies in hardback and was translated into 6 different languages. She wrote continuously throughout her life, writing bestsellers for an astonishing 76 years. Her books have always been immensely popular in the United States, where in 1976 her current books were at numbers 1 & 2 in the B. Dalton bestsellers list, a feat never achieved before or since by any author.

Barbara Cartland became a legend in her own lifetime and will be best remembered for her wonderful romantic novels, so loved by her millions of readers throughout the world.

Her books will always be treasured for their moral message, her pure and innocent heroines, her good looking and dashing heroes and above all her belief that the power of love is more important than anything else in everyone's life.

*"Flowers have always been an important part of my life. Their beauty and serenity are a constant inspiration and for me to look at the full bloom of a pure untouched rose is to glimpse a little piece of Heaven."*

Barbara Cartland

# CHAPTER ONE
# 1880

Lady Rosella Ryland reached out her hand to gently touch the glorious pink rose hanging down from the trellis above her head.

It was such a perfect shape with its cluster of curled petals, the most beautiful flower on the old rambling rose bush that had been there as long as she could remember.

"Happy birthday Rosella," she whispered sadly to herself, as she breathed in the divine scent of the rose in the warm summer air of the walled garden at New Hall.

It was the first of June and she had just become seventeen years old.

But there was no one to remember that this was a very special day, for her beloved Aunt Beatrice, who had brought her up, was dead and she had no other close family who might wish her a happy birthday or send her a present or even a card with their good wishes.

"Your Ladyship."

There was a crunch of boots on the path behind Rosella. Thomas, the gardener's boy was hurrying towards her with a shallow basket over his arm.

Dear Thomas – *he* had remembered what day it was and he was bringing her a present.

But as he came closer, she saw that the basket was empty except for a pair of secateurs.

"I thought you might like – " Thomas stammered, looking shyly at her from under the fair hair that hung over his forehead like a pony's mane, " – to cut some of the flowers, like you used to, my Lady."

Rosella could not help the tears that stung her eyes.

It was not that Thomas had forgotten her birthday. After all, he was just the gardener's boy! Why should he have remembered that today was such a special occasion for her?

The staff at New Hall had been deeply shocked by her aunt's sudden death and were most preoccupied with what might happen to them in the future, as Lord Carlton Brockley, Lady Beatrice's brother, would be coming soon to take up residence and no one knew what kind of a man he might be to work for.

Thomas would be no exception to that, of course. He might even fear that he would lose his job.

No – it was not the fact that he had not wished Rosella 'happy birthday'. It was the memory of so many happy times she had spent in the walled garden, gathering flowers to take to her aunt, that suddenly caused Rosella's heart to ache.

Every morning she used to cut some of the finest blooms of whichever flowers were in season and take them to her aunt, where she sat on the yellow silk sofa in the drawing room after breakfast with her constant companion, Pickle, the grey parrot, in his cage by her side.

As Rosella stood there in the bright sunshine on her birthday, struggling to hold back her tears, she remembered another day, just one month before, when she had hurried back to The Hall through a shower of soft spring rain, her arms full of white lilac and huge crimson peonies.

"*Hello, hello! Good morning, my dear!*" Pickle called out from his cage, as she entered the drawing room, ruffling his grey feathers and holding his head on one side to stare at her.

"Why, why, it's my darling Rosella!" Aunt Beatrice exclaimed. "What a wonderful choice. The scent of lilac reminds me that summer will soon be here and the white flowers will look so very pretty next to the red peonies. How clever you are."

That day Rosella's aunt was in her usual place on the yellow sofa, but she was not sitting there. She had put her feet up and was lying back on the cushions as if she was very tired.

But she was smiling and seemed so pleased with the flowers that Rosella thought nothing of it.

The parlourmaid brought a big blue-and-white vase and scissors and Rosella began to arrange the flowers.

"Just think," Aunt Beatrice said dreamily. "in a few short weeks the garden will be full of roses again,"

"Your favourite flower," Rosella replied, trimming the stem of a lilac branch. "And mine, too, naturally."

"I should hope so!" her aunt smiled.

It was a favourite little joke of theirs – for Rosella had been named after her Mama, whose first name was Ella and after her Papa's favourite flower – the rose.

"There are lots of buds already on the rose bushes," Rosella said now. "There will be masses of flowers soon."

"Oh – I just cannot wait." Then Aunt Beatrice gave a little sigh. "This garden here at New Hall, I am so lucky to have enjoyed it all these years. It must be the finest in all of Hampshire. At least that is what your dear Papa, my darling brother, always told me when he came to visit."

Rosella looked up from the flowers, as she heard her aunt give another little sigh.

"Did I come with him too?" she asked, trying to think of something cheerful to say, as her aunt's elegant head was bowed, as if she was about to cry.

"Oh yes, my darling. As soon as you could put one foot in front of the other, you used to totter up and down the paths following your Papa."

Aunt Beatrice's eyes were shining brightly again as her mind travelled back in time.

"You tried so hard to copy him, when he told you the names of some of the roses, *Gloire de Dijon – Cardinal Richelieu*, but the words were much too hard for you."

"I know them all now. Every single one!"

"He would have been proud of you," Aunt Beatrice said. "Very very proud."

And she shook her head, looking sad again.

Rosella's Mama and Papa, Lord and Lady Ryland had died in Italy in a railway accident, when she was still a tiny child.

She could hardly remember them, but sometimes the echo of her Mama's soft voice and the strong feel of her Papa's hand holding hers would come to her when she was alone in the garden, walking along the same paths they had explored all those years ago.

Aunt Beatrice had brought her up, here at New Hall – the beautiful Georgian house that was not new anymore at all, but was almost a hundred years old.

"You are my greatest blessing, Rosella," her aunt had told her many times. "What a very sad and lonely life I would have had without you – "

Sadly Lord Peregrine Brockley, Aunt Beatrice's husband, had passed away not long after they were married and before any children had been born to them.

When her brother and sister-in-law died, leaving their little daughter penniless and without a home, since the Ryland estate had passed to a distant elderly male cousin, who had no liking for small children, Aunt Beatrice had no hesitation in taking in her niece and loving her as if she was her own child.

Now Rosella had finished arranging the lilac and peonies and she lifted up the heavy vase to show her aunt.

"Oh, darling. How marvellous."

The bright June sun shone in through the window, its bright rays falling on her aunt as she lay on the sofa.

"Aunt Beatrice – " Rosella said, her heart feeling full of a strange anxious pain she had never felt before, as she noticed the dark shadows beneath her aunt's eyes, "are you feeling quite all right? You look very tired."

"I am absolutely fine. I have been a little short of breath these last few days. But do you know something? Talking of the roses has reminded me of something very important indeed."

She sat up on the sofa, moving out of the bright patch of sunlight.

"Darling, please go to the bureau and bring me the little silver bag that is in the drawer."

Rosella did as she was told.

Her aunt's silver mesh purse felt heavy in her hands as she carried it back to the sofa.

"Now then."

Aunt Beatrice undid the clasp.

"Your birthday! I cannot quite believe it, but you are going to be seventeen years old. My darling little girl is all of a sudden quite grown-up."

She tipped the purse upside down and a cascade of gold coins poured onto the little table beside the sofa.

"There. I think that should be more than enough to buy the loveliest dress we can find for the prettiest girl in Hampshire, don't you?"

"Oh! Aunt Beatrice, what a lot of money!"

Rosella had never seen so many coins, all piled up together.

"No expense shall be spared, my darling – "

She was about to say something else, but her voice caught in her throat and she gave a little cough.

"What is it?"

Rosella felt anxious again, as she saw that her aunt was pressing her hand to her side.

"Nothing. Nothing at all."

Aunt Beatrice shook her head and, gathering up the coins, dropped them back in the purse.

"Here, my darling. Take this and keep it very safe. And as soon as I am feeling a bit brighter, we shall go into Winchester to the dressmaker. How would you like that?"

"I – think it would be lovely."

Rosella felt very awkward. It did not seem right to take the purse with all that money inside, but her aunt was thrusting it into her hand.

"I have been putting these sovereigns aside for you for a long time," she said. "Take them. They are yours."

And then she lay back and closed her eyes.

"My darling, I really am feeling a little bit under the weather today. Please would you ask the maid to bring me a cup of tea? And then I think I will rest until luncheon."

Now, standing under the rose trellis in the hot June sunshine, Rosella shivered, remembering that day and the one that followed.

Aunt Beatrice had not come into luncheon.

She had retired to her bedroom and, although she got up the next day as usual, when Rosella brought a bunch of pink-and-white striped tulips to her in the drawing room, she did not move or speak when Rosella approached her, but lay quite still with a gentle smile on her face.

She had passed away as she was sitting in the warm sunlight that streamed in through the window.

"Don't fret, my dear, don't fret." Mrs. Dawkins, the housekeeper, had told Rosella, patting her kindly on the shoulder. "That's a good way to go, why – her Ladyship would hardly have known a thing, so peaceful and happy in the sunshine here and knowing you would be in to her with the flowers in just a moment. Don't grieve for her, my dear. We might all wish for so good an end."

Mrs. Dawkins's grey eyes were bright with tears as she spoke. Rosella could hardly bear to remember the sad expression on the housekeeper's face.

And it still upset her terribly to recall the way that Pickle had called out "*bye bye*" in a sad little voice, as she carried his cage out of the drawing room, almost as if he understood what had happened.

"Your Ladyship?"

The soft Hampshire burr of Thomas's deep voice sounded in Rosella's ears, bringing her back to the present and she became aware again of the strong scent of the pink rose blooms.

"Are you all right?"

"Yes, yes, of course I am. It's so warm today."

Rosella quickly passed a hand over her eyes to wipe away any tears.

"Yes, my Lady. But it's June, so I suppose that we should expect it. Oh – "

He looked down, blushing under his thick fringe of hair.

"What is it?"

"My Lady. I forgot it must be your birthday."

"Oh, Thomas, please don't worry about that."

Rosella's heart gave a little skip – someone had remembered after all!

"Go back to The Hall, my Lady, and I'll bring the flowers to you," he said, his face brightening up. "I knows how it is when there's no family to think about you on your birthday. I've only my sister now and she's in London."

He then picked up the secateurs and began clipping some of the glorious blooms and laying them in the basket.

Rosella strolled back through the bright sunshine to the front door of The Hall and she was just stepping inside when Thomas caught up with her, holding out the basket that was brimming over with pink, white and golden roses.

"Many happy returns for today, my Lady," he said, as he ducked his head in a little bow.

"Oh, my goodness!" squealed Mrs. Dawkins, who had just come into the hall.

"I had quite forgotten! Come Lady Rosella, we must make a big fuss of you."

She took the basket of flowers and led the way to the parlour, a small room where Rosella preferred to sit now, since the drawing room held such sad memories.

"My Lady, I shall put these in water for you and bring you some of your favourite hot chocolate."

Rosella sat in one of the armchairs by the fire.

It was strange to have someone else do for her what she had always done for her aunt.

But when Mrs. Dawkins returned with the roses in a tall glass vase, they looked so lovely she almost forgot how sad she was feeling.

And when the housekeeper set the vase down next to Pickle, who was sitting in his cage on the windowsill, he called out "*goodness gracious*" in such a surprised tone that Rosella had to laugh at him.

"Now, my Lady – "

Mrs. Dawkins watched the parlourmaid coming in with a cup of steaming hot chocolate, before continuing,

"I well know that your dear aunt had planned a very happy day for you. She told me many a time she wanted to take you and buy you a fine gown."

"Yes, that's right, Mrs. Dawkins." Rosella replied. "She even gave me some money, but – I don't think – "

"Well," Mrs. Dawkins was determined to speak her mind. "I know how much your aunt wanted you to have that gown, my Lady, so I am going to call for the carriage to take you into Winchester. And you must then choose the loveliest silk and ask the dressmaker to make you the finest outfit you've ever had!"

Rosella shook her head.

"I couldn't."

"It's what your aunt would have wanted. For her sake, Lady Rosella, you must do it!"

Mrs. Dawkins stood her ground firmly until Rosella finally nodded in agreement and then the kind housekeeper hurried away to speak to the coachman.

*

Mr. Algernon Merriman lounged back against the leather cushions of the Brockley coach, as it jolted along the bumpy country road and wished he had suggested to his friend, Lord Carlton Brockley, that he should use the open landau instead for their journey down to Hampshire.

It would have been much more comfortable on this hot and stuffy day than the cramped interior of the coach.

He looked across at Lord Brockley, who was sitting opposite him and thought that his companion was looking very much the worse for wear.

His Lordship's heavy face, with its drooping jowls and thick black mutton-chop whiskers, was flushed with heat and shiny with sweat.

"Whose idea was this?" Lord Brockley growled, running the back of his hand over his brows. "We would have made much better time on the railway."

"Now then your Lordship. One must keep up one's appearances."

Algernon pulled himself up on the seat so that he was sitting up properly.

He caught a glimpse of his reflected face in the small window above Lord Brockley's head.

They were neither of them getting any younger, but at least he, Algernon, had a good thick head of fair hair still and his long pointed moustache, newly trimmed and waxed by his valet early that morning was perfection!

Luckily his reflection in the little window was not a very good one, so that the nasty black eye he had acquired a few days before, in most embarrassing circumstances, did not show up.

"You are taking possession of your new country residence, Carlton," he continued. "You can't just turn up in the Stationmaster's dog cart like any old passenger. You must make an impression! Arrive in your coach, my Lord, with your coat-of-arms and your coachman, if you please."

"Hah!" Lord Brockley was not at all convinced. He rapped on the roof and shouted out, "how much further?"

"It be just ten miles to the other side of Winchester, sir, we'll soon be there," came the muffled reply.

His Lordship growled impatiently.

"Ten miles too far," he muttered.

"But just think of what awaits you," Algernon said. "One of the most attractive seats in Hampshire, so I am told. Frankly, old man, I can't understand why you haven't claimed it long ago. It's been yours for years."

If he had been lucky enough to inherit a country estate from his elder brother, Albert Merriman – which was about as likely as the prospect of seeing a large pig with wings flashing past the carriage window, since he was only the fourth son of Sir Walgrave Merriman.

His three elder brothers, who were all in excellent health, would have to be out of the way before the family Manor House in Gloucestershire could be his and he would certainly not have allowed his sister-in-law to live there in the lap of luxury for several decades.

All that Algernon had managed to acquire in the way of property was a lease on a small flat in Bayswater, very insufficient for a gentleman such as himself, he felt.

Lord Brockley was in a very different position.

His Lordship had both a fine town house in London and another large country property at Epsom, which was most convenient, since it was right by the Racecourse and so not too far from the City.

It was only the death of his sister-in-law, Beatrice, and the recent decision of his wife to ban him from the London house, that had persuaded him to go to Hampshire.

He pulled a most unpleasant face and grunted,

"What? With the old battleaxe, Beatrice, my sister-in-law still hanging around? No fear! Women! The bane of my life, Merriman, bane of my life! Want nothing to do with them, to be honest with you. Now Beatrice's gone – there'll be no problems."

The fair sex was a very sensitive subject with Lord Brockley just at that very moment.

Relations with his wife, Lady Brockley, had never been particularly cordial, but after the deplorable incident of just a few days ago, she had gone, most unnecessarily, in Algernon's opinion, on the warpath and forbidden her husband entry to the Mayfair house.

Lord Brockley had been reduced to sleeping at his Club, which had led to his spending a great deal of time in the smoking room there and thus the plan to travel down to Hampshire and take possession of New Hall.

"New Hall – new start, your Lordship! What could be better?" Algernon had suggested, thinking that the more miles they could put between themselves and the furious Lady Brockley the better.

In spite of the sweat that was dripping from him in the sweltering interior of the coach, Algernon gave a little shiver as he remembered the expression of icy fury on that Lady's aristocratic countenance and the sheer hatred that blazed from her steely eyes as she ejected both him and Lord Brockley from the front door of the Mayfair House.

"Where is our son?" she had hissed at her husband. "You have driven him away, you useless man! What have you done, you and that despicable friend of yours, to cause him such distress? Get out! And never let me see you here again."

Algernon had tried to protest that it was surely her beloved offspring, Lyndon Brockley, who was at fault and why, he, Algernon, could hardly see at all out of the eye the young man had so impetuously shoved his fist into!

But Lady Brockley was having none of it and the elegant blue door slammed irrevocably shut behind them.

Algernon sighed.

What could he do, when young ladies found him so irresistibly attractive?

He knew that he always looked very dapper in his evening dress, especially the frock coat very cleverly cut to disguise a waistline that had, alas, begun to expand a little in recent years.

And the combined effect of his good tailoring, well-brushed hair and perfectly tweaked moustache had indeed worked its magic on the slightly tipsy young person in the blue dress, who had fallen into his arms on the stairs after dinner at the Brockley's Mayfair house a few nights ago.

A most charming creature and pure chance that she just happened to be engaged to Lyndon, Lord Brockley's son.

If only young Lyndon had then been a little more attentive, he might have been the one to catch her, when her foot became tangled in the train of her dress and the one who should have pressed his lips against her delicious young mouth.

"Merriman!" Lord Brockley's angry voice recalled his companion to the jolting coach. "I cannot continue. I require some liquid refreshment. Immediately!"

One of the reasons why Algernon had remained so close to Lord Brockley for so long, was his willingness to fit in with whatever his Lordship wanted to do.

Now, as he peered out of the window, he could see that they were driving by houses and shop fronts.

"I think we must be in Winchester," he said. "Let's pause at the nearest hostelry."

He reached up and thumped on the roof, shouting to the coachman to take them to an inn.

He was very thirsty himself and a flagon or two or even three of the finest local ale would not go amiss.

As the coach lurched to a halt, Algernon hurriedly fastened up the top button of the riding breeches he had worn for this journey into the country.

He had not worn them for ages and they really were far too tight for him now and most uncomfortable around his middle if he had to sit down for a long period of time.

But one must look the part of a country gentleman if one was to make the right impression on the pretty young girls who might be found in this rural locality.

Girls, like the delightful example he could see now, as he stepped out of the coach.

A slender little thing in a dark gown with the most sublime head of golden curls over which she was holding a parasol, was just walking out of the inn yard and up the High Street.

Lord Brockley stumbled down from the coach.

"Come on, Merriman," he said impatiently. "Leave off chasing the girls for just one day, can't you? This place looks most inviting."

He peered into the interior of the inn and sniffed appreciatively at the mixed aromas of beer and roast beef.

"Merriman, we need go on no further," he insisted with great determination. "I have had enough of travelling and botheration. We will stay here and have a good dinner and go on to New Hall later when we are fully refreshed."

With a lingering glance at the graceful silhouette of the lovely golden-haired girl, now folding up her parasol and disappearing into a shop, Algernon Merriman tipped his hat over his forehead to disguise his huge black eye and followed his companion into the inn.

# CHAPTER TWO

The gown in the window of Palmer's Modes for Ladies was the most beautiful Rosella had ever seen.

It was a pale ivory silk evening dress with a wide flowing skirt, a blue velvet sash and narrow bands of velvet ribbon decorating the bodice.

As she stood on the hot sunny pavement and gazed at it, she thought that it looked like a beautiful white lily growing in a shady corner of the garden.

It was certainly a very pleasant sight after the hustle and bustle of *The Peacock Inn*, where she had just left the carriage.

She had felt quite uncomfortable alighting there, a young girl all on her own and it seemed as if all the ostlers and pot-boys had stopped their work to stare at her.

And then a large covered coach had arrived with two rather disreputable-looking middle-aged men inside – and one of them, a stout fair-haired man with a moustache, had winked at her, which she did not like at all.

A loud jingling noise called Rosella to the present moment, as the door of the dressmaker's shop opened.

"Lady Rosella! What a very pleasant surprise. Will you come inside?"

Mrs. Palmer, who ran the shop, peered at Rosella over her little half-moon glasses.

Rosella folded up her parasol and stepped into the shadowy interior of the shop, which had a pleasant smell of woollen cloth and freshly ironed cotton.

Mrs. Palmer brought a chair for Rosella and offered her a glass of lemonade.

Rosella accepted gratefully and, as she was sipping the cool drink, Mrs. Palmer spoke of Lady Beatrice and what a sad loss she was to the town and local villages.

"Her Ladyship will be so missed," she sighed.

Rosella explained about the money her aunt had given her to buy a gown and Mrs. Palmer's eyes lit up.

"I saw you looking, your Ladyship, at the model in the window! You will be needing a pretty evening gown like that, as I am sure you will have many balls to attend, now that you have become a young lady."

She hurried into the rear of the shop and came back with an armful of silks of all different colours.

There were endless purples and violets and lilacs, yellows and golds and several different shades of pink, ranging from the palest of pearly sheen to a bright vivid colour like a fuchsia flower.

Mrs. Palmer slid the large bolts of silk onto a chair.

"There!" she said. "And if you cannot see what you like, my Lady, I have plenty more to choose from."

Rosella could not help reaching out to touch one of the bolts of silk. It was the colour of a pink rose petal.

"Ah!" the dressmaker smiled. "What good taste you have, my Lady. And may I suggest this for the trimming?"

She then pulled a bunch of cherry-coloured velvet ribbons from a box.

"I-I'm not sure," Rosella hesitated.

The colours looked quite perfect together, but she could not imagine herself wearing them.

All her dresses at New Hall were either white or pale blue, most suitable for a young girl. And, now, since her aunt's death, she had grown used to wearing the dark colours of mourning and even though it was her favourite colour, she had never worn a pink gown.

"Why – but you have just the complexion to carry off this combination."

Mrs. Palmer extended a hand to Rosella.

"Come to the mirror over here and I'll show you."

The dressmaker unfurled several yards of the pink silk and folded it round Rosella and then held up the bright ribbons at her waist and neck.

Rosella gasped.

In the mirror in front of her, she saw a tall and beautiful woman with lengths of golden hair tumbling over her bare shoulders and dressed in the glorious colours of a midsummer rose.

"Who – ?" Rosella whispered, looking over her shoulder, for she thought that this woman must have come silently into the shop and come to stand beside her.

But, of course, it was herself there in the mirror, just a slim shy girl trying out some silks for their colour.

She stared at her reflection and suddenly the mirror seemed to ripple in front of her and instead of the cramped dress shop, she could see a vast gloomy hall and a huge chandelier winking with candle flames hanging down from a high vaulted ceiling.

The beautiful woman stepped back, her pink skirts ruffling around her feet and Rosella saw that she wore a black velvet mask covered in tiny diamonds over her eyes.

And all round this woman shadowy figures moved, joining hands and then parting, as if going through all the steps of a dance.

And now the woman turned away, as if someone was approaching her and, as she lifted her hand to take the mask from her face, Rosella saw the figure of a tall man step out of the shadows, and she felt her heart swell inside her with a feeling that was half-excitement and half-fear, so that she could scarcely breathe.

"What is it, your Ladyship? Are you all right?"

Mrs. Palmer's voice sounded faintly in her ears, but Rosella could hardly hear her, for now her head was full of the sound of violins and other strings, playing a swirling, passionate tune that made her heart beat even faster.

And then the mirror rippled again, the pink-clad figure faded away and Rosella shivered as the shelves and the counter of the dressmaker's shop spun around her and the low ceiling seemed to loom down over her head.

The floor was rocking under her feet and suddenly there was a bump and her cheek was pressed against the rough wool of the carpet.

From very far away, she could now hear someone calling her name and then she felt a burning sensation in her nose and she realised that she had fallen down in a faint and that Mrs. Palmer was holding a vial of smelling salts in front of her face.

"Oh – " Rosella gasped, struggling to sit up. "Oh, I am so sorry."

"Please, my Lady. Don't rush or you will bring on another faint."

Mrs. Palmer put her arm round Rosella's shoulders and held the glass of cold lemonade to her forehead.

"This hot weather is so trying," she added, looking very anxious.

Rosella closed her eyes, attempting to recapture the strange scene in the mirror.

The music still echoed in her ears and, now that Mrs. Palmer had removed the smelling salts, a mysterious, cool scent, like river water, was filling her nose.

But the vast hall and the candles had all vanished, along with the woman in the glorious pink gown.

"Shall I send for your carriage, my Lady?" Mrs. Palmer asked, bending over her.

Very slowly Rosella rose to her feet.

"Thank you, Mrs. Palmer, but I am sure I will be able to walk to *The Peacock Inn*. It is only just down the High Street and that is where my carriage is waiting."

Mrs. Palmer bent down and gathered up the folds of pink silk that lay shining at their feet.

Somehow the sight of the silk made Rosella feel uneasy. It was her favourite colour, but it was almost too beautiful to look at and she could not help but think of the strange vision she had just seen in the mirror.

Mrs. Palmer insisted that she should walk with her, in case she became unwell again.

"No, please don't trouble. The fresh air will revive me, I am sure." Rosella said. "Thank you so much for looking after me. I will come back in a few days' time and choose a new dress for myself."

She then put up her parasol and walked out into the bright sunlight on the High Street.

The voices of the passers-by seemed very loud and the dust that the passing horses kicked up from the road as they trotted by stung her eyes.

It was good to be outside again, but Rosella was still not feeling quite herself.

She could not get the dreamlike vision she had just experienced out of her mind and she longed to go home and lie down on her bed, close her eyes and see if she could conjure up that vast gloomy hall and the soft light of the chandelier again.

When she arrived at *The Peacock Inn* and walked under the arch that led from the High Street into the yard, there was no one about.

The carriage was there, next to the wall, but the horses had been put away in the stable and the coachman was nowhere to be seen.

Suddenly Rosella was startled by a load roar of excited men's voices from inside the inn.

She could hear cheers and shouts of "yes, by Jove! He's done it!"

Everyone must have gone inside, so she walked up to the door and looked in and all she could see was a crowd of men with their backs to her.

Gentlemen in well-cut riding coats, brawny ostlers in dusty leather aprons and baggy cord trousers and stable boys with straw in their hair, all jostling to get the best view of a table in the corner.

Suddenly the place became completely silent, as if everyone was holding his breath in anticipation.

Rosella heard the rattle of dice being shaken and thrown over the table and another huge roar filled the inn.

"He's got the luck of the Devil!" someone shouted.

There was a scrape of chairs from the corner table and Rosella saw the gentleman with the moustache, who had winked at her earlier, sitting there playing dice.

He stood up now, his round face flushed red with excitement.

"I'd better stop," he cried with a loud laugh, "or I'll bankrupt the lot of you! What a marvellous run of luck. Fifty pounds on a few throws of the dice!"

He scooped up a pile of coins from the table.

"A round of your best ale for everyone!" he shouted to the innkeeper, who was watching from behind the bar.

Then he looked across and saw Rosella standing by the door.

"Who's this?" he asked, his small eyes glinting at her. "Could it be Lady Luck herself? Is it this pretty little angel who's making the dice fall my way?"

Rosella backed towards the door, blushing fiercely.

Whatever did he mean? She had no interest at all in the dice game and, to her horror, all the men were looking at her now and laughing.

"Hey there!" the man with the moustache called. "Don't you run away now, sweetheart. Stay and bring me more luck!"

The others were shouting out to her too, telling her to stay.

She looked around in desperation for her coachman and saw that he was making his way towards her through the crowd, a tankard of beer in his hand.

"Forgive me, my Lady," he said, looking rather shamefaced. "I just couldn't 'elp but drink 'is Lordship's 'ealth."

But Rosella did not listen to what he was saying.

"Please, I wish to go back to New Hall at once," she told him, as she was desperate to escape from the hot and crowded inn.

"Of course, my Lady."

The coachman set his tankard down on a table.

"I'll bring them 'orses right away."

And he hurried off towards the stables.

Now the man with the moustache was being lifted up by several ostlers so that he was standing on the bar.

"I should like," he began and swayed a little to one side. "I should like to drink to my very lovely little angel over there who's been helping me to win so much money!"

He took another large gulp from his glass of beer and continued drunkenly,

"And I mustn't forget to propose a toast to – the man who brought me here to this delightful inn and who suggested a little game of dice before luncheon. My very good friend – here's to his Lordship!"

Another cheer rent the air and everyone raised his glass or his tankard to join the fair-haired man's toast.

And then Rosella saw that there was another man who had been sitting at the corner table, a man with thick mutton-chop whiskers.

Rosella thought he must have been very handsome once, as he had strong aristocratic features. But now his hair was streaked with grey and his cheeks were lined and heavy, giving him a bad-tempered expression.

'This must be 'his Lordship',' Rosella thought, as the man raised a hand in acknowledgement of those who were toasting him.

Then a waiter brought him a large platter of meat and vegetables and the irritable-looking Lord bent his head over it and began to shovel the food into this mouth.

With relief Rosella heard the coachman calling her name from the yard outside. The horses were harnessed up and the coach was ready for her to depart.

"Well, my Lady, there'll be some surprised faces back at New Hall when they 'ear our news," the coachman said, as he gave her his arm to help her up into the coach.

Rosella did not take notice of what he was saying. She only wanted to return home and retire to the peaceful sanctuary of her bedroom.

As the carriage swayed along the graceful country lanes, Rosella lay back on the cushions, closed her eyes and tried to picture again the masked woman in the pink dress and the mysterious stranger who had approached her from the shadows of the vast ballroom.

Who was he?

She had only caught the very merest glimpse of him when she had the strange vision in the shop, but if she kept trying, she might just be able to remember his face.

"Lady Rosella!"

The coach had come to a halt and someone was opening the door.

Rosella blinked and saw Mrs. Dawkins gazing at her anxiously.

The housekeeper's face was now flushed and her normally immaculate white cap was slipping sideways as if it had been caught in a high wind.

"Are you feeling quite all right, your ladyship?" she asked. "I can't believe that you have drifted off to sleep! Why, the coachman has only just told me who has come to town and who will be here at New Hall very shortly."

"What? I don't – " Rosella stammered.

"*Lord Brockley!*" Mrs. Dawkins exclaimed. "He's here! He's come to Hampshire without letting us know. And the coachman says he's taking his luncheon at the inn and he'll be here for tea! How we shall get everything ready for him in time, I really don't know."

Rosella's heart seemed to turn right over.

"Did you see him?" Mrs. Dawkins asked, her hand on Rosella's arm. "What was he like?"

"I just couldn't say," Rosella replied, picturing the man with the mutton-chop whiskers wolfing down his plate of food at the inn. "I think I saw him, and – he seemed a distinguished-looking man, but I did not speak to him."

"Distinguished-looking. Oh, my!" Mrs. Dawkins' eyes were bright with excitement. "I must get back to the laundry and make sure that the maids have ironed enough sheets. The coachman says that his Lordship has brought a gentleman with him from London for company."

Rosella's heart felt a sudden chill.

Not only would there be a new Master at New Hall – and one who did not look like a kind and pleasant man, but the other gentleman, who had so rudely shouted at her in the bar of the inn, would be coming with him.

Her despondency must have showed on her face, as Mrs. Dawkins apologised for asking so many questions.

"Your Ladyship, I am being quite out of order," she said, straightening her cap. "You must be hungry after your trip into town. I will order luncheon for you directly."

"Please don't bother, Mrs. Dawkins. It's such a hot day and I really am not hungry at all. I shall go up to my room and lie down for a little."

"And be sure to put on one of your prettiest gowns for tea," the housekeeper added, as she hurried away to the laundry.

There was no one but Pickle, who was sitting in his cage in the drawing room, to hear how unhappy Rosella was feeling and he was just settling down on his perch for his afternoon nap, tucking his head under his grey wing.

She left him to doze in peace and ran up the stairs to her bedroom.

She tossed her parasol onto the bed and was just about to take her shoes off to lie down, when one of the pictures on her bedroom wall caught her eye.

It was a portrait of a young man, not much more than a boy, wearing a cloth wrapped around his head like a turban and a blue jacket and trousers sewn all over with little jewels.

This portrait had been in Rosella's family for many years. It had been given to her Papa by her grandfather.

She had asked many times who the young man was, but no one could tell her. Aunt Beatrice had thought that Grandpapa might have brought the painting back from one of his travels in Italy, but that was all she knew about it.

Rosella liked the portrait so much that she had been allowed to keep it in her bedroom.

Even as a little child she had loved the way that the young man was smiling broadly and how he seemed to be beckoning with his hand, as if inviting her to step inside the picture and join him.

But this time, as she looked at him, her heart was racing with excitement.

For, just behind the young man's head, she could see the painted outline of a huge chandelier – just like the one she had seen in her vision.

And now, as she jumped up to look more closely, she realised that the young man in the turban was standing in the very same ballroom where she had seen the beautiful woman in the pink dress!

"Oh, goodness! How strange all this is!" she cried, gazing at his face. "If only you could talk to me. Who are you? And where are you?"

His smiling lips looked as if they were about to open and speak to her. But, of course, he was just a picture and, although she waited a while, he could tell her nothing.

Rosella turned away and went to lie down.

*

The smells wafting from the slow-moving waters of the River Thames and drifting between the high walls of the nearby warehouses were strong and unpleasant on this very hot afternoon and Lord Lyndon Brockley entered the narrow doorway of the pawnshop with some relief.

"Yes, sir?" the bent old man behind the counter looked up at him with interest.

Lyndon gazed at the racks of coats and cloaks that hung behind the old man and at the glass case full of gold chains and brooches and shiny pocket watches.

He had never been inside a pawnshop before and he had just thought it might be a useful place for him to pick up a change of clothes – a disguise – so that if he bumped into anyone he knew, they would not recognise him.

He had not really thought of all the people who had fallen on hard times and who had come here to pawn not just their valuables but even their clothes for a little cash.

How many of these people, he thought, would ever be able to come back and claim their possessions?

There was a sad smell of poverty and unwashed shirts lingering in the shop and he turned to leave.

"Hold on, sir," the old man called out. "What is it you need? All sorts come here for our help."

Lyndon shook his head.

"Nothing, really. I made a mistake."

The shop door rattled and a thin young girl came in, her arms piled high with a mass of black garments.

Lyndon stood back to let her pass and she went up to the counter and dumped the clothes on it.

"There!" she said. "What'll you give me for 'em?"

Lyndon noticed that the garments, coats and jackets and trousers of black wool looked old but well made.

The old man shook his head.

"Where did all these come from?"

"The Mistress gave me them."

"A fine story," the old man retorted. "Next thing I know, I'll have the Constable here going through my stuff and doing me for handling stolen goods. Be off with you!"

"But – " the girl's grey eyes filled with tears.

"Out!"

The old man then shoved the pile of clothes off the counter, pushing them at the girl so that she staggered and almost fell.

Lyndon caught the girl's arm to steady her and then followed as she stumbled out onto the street.

"Are you all right?" he asked her, as she seemed so upset.

"The Master died last night, bless 'im, poor old thing," she sighed and gave a little sob. "And the Mistress said I should take 'is clothes, as she don't want 'em in the 'ouse no more."

Lyndon noticed that the girl was wearing a white parlourmaid's apron and cap.

"Who is – was – your Master?" he asked her.

"Signore Goldoni!" she replied and a large tear slid down her thin cheek. "The best violin player you've ever 'eard, till he got poorly and took to 'is bed."

She must be telling the truth, Lyndon thought.

"Don't you have a family that you could give them to?" he asked her. "Your Papa or a brother perhaps might like them?"

She gave a squeak of laughter through her tears.

"What for? These are gentlemen's things. Look at this great black cloak. I can't see me Pa wearin' that when 'e goes to the docks to look for work. And me brothers are just little 'uns still. No we need the money, mister. Ma's just got a new baby and Pa's bin laid up with a bad back. They must be worth a bit."

Lyndon took the black cloak from the top of the pile and held it up. It was very long and fastened at the neck with a loop of thick gold chain.

27

No one would recognise him if he wore something like this.

"Did the Signore wear a hat by any chance?" he asked.

The girl nodded.

"It's 'ere, somewhere," she said. "A great big old floppy thing!"

Lyndon then reached into his pocket and took out a handful of coins.

"Here," he said. "I'll take the things. Please give my best regards to your family – and my condolences to the Signora Goldoni!"

The girl's mouth fell open with astonishment.

"Oh, thank you! Thank you, sir," she cried.

She gave a little curtsy, clutching the money to her heart and her face was so full of delight that Lyndon had no doubt that she was telling the truth about the clothes.

As she hurried away up the narrow street, he looked around at the towering warehouses for a deserted doorway where he might hide and effect his transformation.

There was no time to be lost.

# CHAPTER THREE

"*Hello, hello*! *What shall we have for tea*?" Pickle was squawking, sounding uncannily like Aunt Beatrice.

Rosella smiled and pushed her finger through the bars of his cage so that he could nibble on it with his beak.

The parrot was usually allowed out of his cage at teatime to fly around the drawing room and play hide-and-seek amongst the curtains.

But that did not seem such a good idea today with Lord Brockley and his companion about to arrive. Pickle was nervous with strangers until he became used to them.

It would not be a good introduction to his new Master if he flew up onto the top of the pelmet and would not come down.

"They are very late," Mrs. Dawkins said, standing by the cake stand that she had set down on a small table. "Something must have happened to delay his Lordship."

Next to the cake stand stood a large plate of thin cucumber sandwiches, from which Mrs. Dawkins herself had carefully cut the crusts and they were beginning to curl up in the heat of the afternoon.

Rosella looked at the gold clock on the mantelpiece and saw that it was almost half-past five.

The housekeeper twisted her hands nervously.

"What do you suppose has happened to them?" she moaned. "I do hope that nothing is wrong."

"I am sure his Lordship will be here very soon," Rosella replied encouragingly.

What had happened, she was quite sure, was that someone at the inn had bought another round of beer for everybody and then someone else had done the same thing and this had detained Lord Brockley.

Pickle suddenly shook himself and sneezed loudly,

"*Bless you, my dear*!" he called out.

Rosella laughed at him, then she noticed that he had his head on one side as if he was listening to something.

His hearing was particularly good, often very much sharper than Rosella's and after a moment, she realised that he had now picked up the clatter of hooves in the distance.

"They are coming!" she said and her heart fluttered nervously.

"I shall call the servants out onto the terrace," the housekeeper said, looking pale. "We must all be there to greet his Lordship and you as well, Lady Rosella."

It was very hot out on the terrace in front of The Hall and the maids' white aprons fluttered in the breeze as they stood beside the footmen, the gardeners, the grooms and all the other servants, forming a wide avenue to greet their new Master.

At the very top of the steps, Mrs. Dawkins and Hodgkiss, the ancient butler, took their places by the stone pillars that flanked the front door.

Rosella felt very awkward.

She was not sure where she should stand out there on the hot terrace and was thinking that perhaps she should wait inside in the cool of the hall, when a large coach with the Brockley family coat-of-arms emblazoned on the door careered up the drive at breakneck speed and came to a sudden halt, scattering pellets of gravel everywhere.

Sitting up on the box, clinging tightly to the reins, was the fair-haired man who had winked at Rosella earlier.

"Whoa, there!" he shouted, even though the horses had already come to a standstill. "Mettlesome brutes, hey? But then I've got the measure of them all. That was a fine run, wasn't it, coachman?"

The coachman touched his hat politely.

"Yes, indeed, sir," he murmured.

He was very red in the face and seemed relieved, Rosella thought, when the fair-haired gentleman let him take the reins back into his own hands.

"Is that him?" Mrs. Dawkins whispered to Rosella, staring at the fair-haired gentleman.

But the footman who rode on the back of the coach had jumped down and was opening the door.

The angry man with the mutton-chop whiskers then emerged from the coach, his face like a thundercloud.

"Merriman, you clown!" he growled. "You damn near got us all killed."

Rosella touched Mrs. Dawkins's arm.

"That's Lord Brockley!" she whispered.

His Lordship walked slowly towards the steps that led up to the front door and there was a ripple of white aprons as the maids all dropped into deep curtseys.

Hodgkiss then bent into a respectful bow and Mrs. Dawkins dropped such a low curtsey that she was almost on the ground.

As Lord Brockley mounted the steps, he scowled at Rosella, his dark eyes flashing under his hooded lids.

"What's this?" he grunted. "Get back to your place, miss!"

He jerked his head at Rosella, indicating that she should go down and join the maids.

Then he pushed past, almost knocking her aside and went into the hall with Mrs. Dawkins scurrying after him.

Rosella caught hold of one of the stone pillars to stop herself from falling.

She might be wearing a dark blue dress, but, even so, how could her uncle have mistaken her for a servant? Could he not see she had no apron?

"Out of the way, young lady!"

A blast of beery breath struck Rosella in the face.

The fair-haired gentleman too had staggered up the steps and he went to push past Rosella, muttering,

"We're here just in time, that's for sure. Servants soon get above their rightful place when there's no Master in the house!"

Then he gave a violent hiccup and grabbed at the stone pillar to steady himself.

"Pardon me!" he said and then his little blue eyes grew wide with surprise. "Well! This really is my lucky day. It's the divine little angel from the inn!"

He reached out as if to catch Rosella's hand, but she backed away and he swayed on his feet and almost fell.

She longed to run away, but she must not be rude to this gentleman, her uncle's friend, so she smiled politely at him and said,

"Welcome, sir, to New Hall. I am Lady Rosella Ryland, the niece of Lady Beatrice."

His eyes looked as if they would pop out of his head.

"Well I never!"

He then made a wobbly bow, almost overbalancing.

"Would you care to step inside?" she said, going into the hall. "Mrs. Dawkins has laid tea for you in the drawing room."

Algernon made a smacking noise with his lips.

"Delightful!" he exclaimed. "And just the ticket. I heartily approve of your Hampshire hospitality. Had a nice taste of it already – at that excellent inn," he added and gave another loud hiccup.

Rosella led him to the drawing room, hearing his unsteady footsteps behind her on the tiled floor.

Lord Brockley was seated in an armchair close to the fireplace with a disparaging look on his dark face.

"Oh, there you are, Merriman," he said, taking no notice at all of Rosella.

Algernon stood by the sofa, swaying a little as he gazed around at the room.

"Marvellous place," he said. "Absolutely top hole, your Lordship."

Lord Brockley sniffed.

"A modest little country seat. My house at Epsom is vastly superior."

It was as if Rosella did not exist.

She looked around anxiously for Mrs. Dawkins, but the housekeeper must have gone to bring a pot of fresh tea.

What should she do? Should she quietly slip away and leave the two gentlemen alone or should she introduce herself to Lord Brockley?

The matter was taken out of her hands.

"Look who I've found," Algernon was now saying. "The little beauty from the inn!"

Lord Brockley scowled.

"What? I let you out of my sight for one moment, Merriman, and you are off chasing some female again."

"Not guilty, your Lordship. This little sweetheart is part of the fixtures and fittings! She's the niece of old Beatrice, your sister-in-law."

Lord Brockley looked annoyed.

"I do remember now, some mention of a girl living here. A useless encumbrance, no doubt, that I must now be responsible for."

Rosella felt her face grow hot with embarrassment, but she was saved from any further unpleasant comments by the arrival of Mrs. Dawkins with a silver teapot.

"Here, my Lord," the housekeeper said and Rosella noticed that the tray was trembling slightly in her hands. "Will you take cream and sugar? And a slice of cake?"

"*Cake!*" A small voice spoke up from the corner of the room, where Pickle's cage stood. "*Yes, please!*"

Lord Brockley did not seem to have noticed a thing, but Algernon looked surprised. From his seat on the sofa, he could not see the parrot's cage.

"What was that?" he asked and then he hiccupped loudly. "Pardon me!"

Rosella was just about to explain about Pickle, but Algernon was now being distracted by Mrs. Dawkins, who was standing by his elbow with the teapot.

"Cream or milk, sir?"

"*Cake!*" Pickle screamed a little more loudly. And then he gave a loud hiccup – exactly like Algernon's.

"Quite enough of that, Merriman!" Lord Brockley muttered. "You are being ridiculous."

"But I – "

Algernon looked rather confused as he accepted a cup of tea from Mrs. Dawkins.

"*Hic!*" Pickle squawked again and gave a raucous laugh. "*Ha ha ha!*"

Lord Brockley's expression was thunderous now.

"Merriman, I am not amused."

Pickle copied his Lordship's angry tone, shouting, "*Stop it!  You naughty boy!*"

Algernon jumped up, spilling his tea on the carpet.

"What the devil – " he began, and then he saw the parrot cage. "It's a talking bird!  A stupid parrot."

He went over to look at Pickle, who jumped off his perch onto the floor of the cage, growling like a dog.

"He isn't used to strangers – " Rosella began, but it was too late.

"Little devil!" Algernon exclaimed.

He poked his finger through the bars of the cage.

Pickle gave a loud scream and bit it.

Algernon then staggered backwards over the carpet, shaking blood from his finger.

"Ouch!" he gasped.

"I'm so – sorry," Rosella stammered, hurrying over to Pickle's cage. "I had better take him out."

"Yes, and shoot the damn thing, while you're at it!" Lord Brockley grunted. "Pull yourself together, old man – it's just a flesh wound."

Algernon collapsed on the sofa, mopping his finger with one of the silk cushions.

Rosella lifted Pickle's cage down from the table.

She must take him out of the room as soon as she could before Lord Brockley became any more irritated.

"Sweetheart." Algernon sighed in a wheedling tone. "I'm wounded.  Leave that horrible bird and tend to me!"

"Pull yourself together, Merriman," Lord Brockley snapped.

Then his Lordship stood up from the armchair and stared at Rosella with his dark hooded eyes and something about his expression sent a little shiver down her spine.

"You seem a good girl, whatever your name is."

"Rosella."

Her voice was shaking, but she hoped that he would not notice.

"Hmm. Modest. Quiet. Sensible."

Lord Brockley's lips twisted in an unpleasant smile.

"Not exactly what I would have expected. No doubt my silly sister-in-law Beatrice spoiled you dreadfully."

"She – was very kind to me."

"I daresay, but she is not here now. We must have a little discussion about your future before too long."

Lord Brockley was still smiling and Rosella could see that his uneven teeth were stained brown from tobacco and wine.

"Go," he said, "and get rid of that wretched bird. I don't wish to see or hear anything of it ever again. You, Rosella, I shall expect to see at dinner."

His eyes glinted at her from under his heavy lids, but he was still smiling, so that she could not tell whether he was angry or amused.

It was difficult to curtsy while holding the heavy birdcage, but Rosella did the best she could and made her way to the door.

Algernon looked up from winding his handkerchief around his hand and gave her a swift wink.

Then he turned to Lord Brockley.

"I need a brandy," he asserted.

Mrs. Dawkins, who had been standing by the door, looked shocked. In all the years she had worked at New Hall, no one had ever asked for brandy in the afternoon.

"Dawkins!" Lord Brockley's harsh voice rang out. "Have the butler bring the best brandy. And a card table. We wish to play."

Mrs. Dawkins nodded and curtseyed, but her grey eyes were full of anxiety as she and Rosella silently left the drawing room.

"*Brandy, Brandy, Brandy!*" Pickle shouted out, as Rosella carried him up the stairs. "*You're a very naughty boy! Give me some cake!*"

"Hush, you bad bird," she whispered, "I don't think there'll be any cake for you today."

She would have to go back into the drawing room to fetch it and she would do anything rather than face Lord Brockley and his friend again.

From now on, she would keep Pickle in her room, for he would come to harm, she was sure, if he caused any more trouble.

Her life at New Hall was certainly going to be very different now that its new owner had taken up residence.

*

The sun had just gone down and a cool breeze was blowing along Piccadilly as Lord Lyndon Brockley strolled along the wide pavement.

The long black cloak swirled around his ankles and the big hat was pulled well down over his forehead.

It was daring of him to come here, but who could possibly recognise him in this Bohemian get-up?

If any of his old school-friends or, worse, any of his Papa's dissolute drinking and gambling associates were to bump into him, they would think he was an eccentric actor, strolling off to an engagement at one of the theatres.

Or perhaps a musician, like Signore Goldoni, the original owner of the cloak and hat – heading to a *café* to play to the assembled diners.

An enticing scent of coffee and newly-baked cakes wafted across the pavement from the open windows of one of the tall hotels that lined the pavement.

37

He had not eaten anything since a hurried breakfast at the inn where he was staying down by the docks and he knew how good the fare was at this particular hotel as he had sampled it many times in the past.

Why should he not go in and sit down at one of the tables and celebrate the ingenious disguise he had found?

It was a daring thought and he longed to carry it out, but he would have to take the hat off once he was inside and that would be too risky.

"Sir?"

The hotel doorman had seen him lingering and was looking at him suspiciously.

'Oh, what the hell! Why not go for it?'

Lyndon took a deep breath and replied, keeping his voice low and adding a slight Mediterranean accent.

"I should like to take some coffee, but I must have a quiet table as I don't wish to be disturbed."

The doorman, who had ushered both Lord Lyndon Brockley and a party of his friends into the hotel only last month, hesitated a moment, as if he was not sure whether this strangely-garbed person should be allowed into such a respectable hotel and then he answered,

"Of course, sir. May I take your hat and er – coat?"

Lyndon shook his head and then was inspired to say in the same accent,

"I must keep them with me. I have been unwell."

The doorman raised his eyebrows.

"Yes. I have recently come from a hot climate and I must not take cold, particularly to the head."

"Of course, sir," the doorman nodded. "India, was it? We will find you a nice quiet corner, sir."

Lyndon's heart beat jubilantly as he walked across the marble floor of the hotel lobby. His ruse had worked and, what was more, the doorman had not recognised him.

The hotel *café* was almost empty as Lyndon settled himself at a small table, which was partly hidden by a large palm tree and ordered some food.

As he ate, several groups of other diners arrived, and, by the time he was drinking his coffee, the *café* was almost full.

It felt good to be in the middle of so much noise and activity with all these people out enjoying themselves, even though Lyndon had to keep himself apart.

But something was making him feel uneasy. There was one voice amongst all the shouts and the laughter that kept nagging at his attention.

A high clear girl's voice, as sweet and melodious as a flute, rang out from a table not too far away,

"Champagne! Julius, you really are too kind."

Marian. It could not be!

Lyndon parted the branches of the palm so that he could peer through.

It *was* her!

His ex-fiancée, sitting a couple of tables away with his best friend from his schooldays, the redheaded rowing champion, Julius Maberley!

Marian looked strikingly beautiful with her glossy brown hair piled up like a Grecian Goddess and her cheeks and lips glowing pink in the light of the candles.

Lyndon felt his heart melting as he watched her.

He had forgotten how exquisitely beautiful she was, with her delicate heart-shaped face and her long eyelashes that fluttered like the wings of a tiny bird.

But what was happening now?

Marian was reaching out across the table to lay her white-gloved hand over Julius's.

Lyndon's heart contracted painfully in his chest.

How could this be? Only a few days ago she had still been insisting that she loved Lyndon and that she was determined to win him back and marry him.

He fumbled in the pocket of the cloak and pulled out a crumpled piece of paper, one of the many letters she had written to him.

*"Darling,*

*You are being an utter fool to make so much fuss about something so silly.*

*Your Papa's good friend, Mr. Merriman, was an absolute poppet – if he hadn't been there on the stairs to catch me, who knows, I might have had a horrible fall.*

*I didn't mean to kiss him, it just sort of happened and anyway, darling, I know you will come round. All girls love to flirt a bit, we just can't help it. It's you I love, Lyndon. There will never be anyone else for me and I shall die if I don't see you.*

*Please, please, darling boy, stop being so silly."*

Lyndon pushed the letter back into his pocket.

Was it really so silly of him to be upset that the girl he loved had allowed one of his Papa's drunken cronies to take her in his arms and then press a horrid lecherous kiss against her lips?

His stomach tied itself in a knot as he remembered Marian's pretty face, laughing at him there on the stairs of his parents' Mayfair home, when he had tried to pull her away from the clutches of Mr. Algernon Merriman.

When he would not see the funny side of it, she had run out of the house, slamming the door behind her.

And then his Papa, sprawling drunkenly across the stair carpet, had yelled at him, told him he was being an idiot and a silly over-sensitive fool.

Even his Mama was not very sympathetic, when he told her what had happened.

"That's just the way your father is," she said, a cold little frown on her aristocratic face. "His mind is only on the next wager he can make."

With a deep sadness and rage, Lyndon realised that she was right and he felt ashamed of his Papa.

"You expect too much of Marian," Lady Brockley continued. "She's a very young and high-spirited girl and there will be a terrible fuss from her family if there is any problem with the engagement."

But Lyndon could not marry a girl who behaved as Marian had done and who did not understand how much she had hurt him.

She did not believe him when he had told her this.

She called at the house in Mayfair, even though he would not speak to her and then she wrote him many letters sometimes three or four a day insisting that she still loved him and that she wanted to marry him as soon as possible.

Thank goodness he had not given in!

As Lyndon watched her through the fronds of the palm tree, he felt the pain in his heart turn to an icy anger.

She was smiling tenderly at his old friend, Julius, and gazing up at him with her huge eyes.

Not so long ago she had looked at Lyndon like that. His instinct had been right. Marian had never truly cared for him.

He had done the right thing by walking out then and there, escaping from his Papa's rudeness, his Mama's

41

coldness, Marian's flirtatious behaviour and the relentless insistence of all of them that he should marry her.

Now Julius had taken Marian's little hand in both of his and was stroking it.

Good old Julius! His very best friend for so many years. How could he betray Lyndon like this?

But he only had to look at Marian, at the reflection of the candle flames making little stars in her dark eyes and her sweet lips parted in a smile, to know why.

Julius had fallen completely under her spell, just as he had done and then something came into Lyndon's mind that cast a chill over his whole body.

Julius came from a very wealthy family indeed. He might not be a Lord, like Lyndon, but his family was even wealthier than the Brockleys.

Perhaps it was not Lyndon that Marian had cared for as much as the houses in Mayfair and Epsom – and the substantial Brockley fortune.

The hubbub of the crowded *café* filled his ears and he felt hot and exhausted.

He pulled the hat from his head and fanned it back and forth to try and make a cool breeze.

Then the palm fronds rustled by him and an angry face topped with a shock of red hair peered through.

"Hey! It's really not on, spying on people like that! I'll have to go and speak to the manager," Julius thundered. "They've no right to let in disreputable types like you."

And then he gasped with shock as he saw Lyndon.

Lyndon clapped the hat back on his head, but it was too late.

Marian was now at Julius's side. She had seen him too.

"If that doesn't beat everything," she exclaimed. "First he won't even speak to me and now he's following me around."

She slid her arm through Julius's and gave Lyndon a proud, cold little smile.

"Come along, darling," she proposed seductively.

Julius stared at Lyndon.

"You'd better leave," he suggested, his face almost as red as his hair.

Lyndon put his hat on with a flourish and dropped a few coins on the table to pay for his food.

"I wish you a pleasant evening," he said and turned his back on them.

The long black cloak swirled around his body as he walked out of the hotel, ignoring the stares of the guests in the lobby.

It was twilight outside now and, as he strode along the pavement, he wanted to keep on walking until London was far behind him.

What was there to stay for?

His friends, his family, the woman he had loved, all meant nothing to him now.

And, in his brand new disguise, he was free to go wherever and be whoever he liked.

All he had to do was decide on a destination.

# CHAPTER FOUR

Through a cloud of cigar smoke, Rosella could see that Mr. Algernon Merriman had fallen forward onto the table and was fast asleep, his cheek resting on his arms.

The flickering candlelight illuminated a bald patch on the crown of his head, which she had not noticed before.

It was a long time since Rosella had dined with any gentlemen at New Hall, as her Aunt Beatrice had very few guests, but she knew that Lord Brockley and Mr. Merriman should leave the table and go to the smoking room to enjoy their port and cigars.

A strange whistling noise, accompanied by a series of loud grunts, came from Algernon. He was snoring.

Rosella could not bear it any longer, so she pushed her chair back and rose to her feet.

"If you will excuse me, my Lord," she began, but Lord Brockley waved his cigar at her, indicating that she should sit down again.

"Where are you going?" he demanded and a ring of smoke escaped from his thin lips, expanding slowly before dissolving into a misty cloud that hung over the table. "We haven't had our little discussion yet."

Rosella's head swam and she felt as if she could not breathe.

"It is very late now, my Lord," she said, thinking longingly of her cool quiet bedroom.

"This is my house," Lord Brockley asserted, "and late or early, while you are staying here, your time is my time."

There was something about the tone of his voice that made Rosella suddenly shiver.

"Your fortune," he continued. "What is it?"

And then he smiled the cold smile she had seen that afternoon, as she lowered herself onto her chair again.

"I – don't have a fortune."

"Nothing?" His bushy eyebrows rose. "Surely you must have *something*."

Rosella was very glad that she was sitting down, as her whole body was trembling now.

"No, my Lord."

She pictured the bag of sovereigns that her aunt had given her, safely locked in the drawer of her dressing table. He must never know of its existence.

"Your family, then. Where are they?"

Lord Brockley's eyes glinted in the candlelight.

"Why did they not come for you when my sister died?"

"I have no family – "

"How can that be?"

He frowned at her.

"My Mama and Papa – died."

Fighting to keep her voice calm and level, Rosella explained about her family estate and how everything had been inherited by her elderly cousin.

"Then you must go to him."

Rosella shook her head.

"He will not help me. He did not want me, when I became – an orphan."

Lord Brockley grunted.

"That is no surprise. Children, nothing but trouble. Even one's own. Well, there is nothing for it. You must find yourself a husband."

Rosella did not know what to say.

"Perhaps you have some young admirer, who will take you off my hands?"

Rosella shook her head.

At that moment Algernon twitched in his sleep and made a loud spluttering noise, throwing out his hand and knocking a wineglass over.

Lord Brockley sighed impatiently.

"I am surrounded by useless fools," he said. "I had fancied a game of cards after dinner. But look at him!"

Rosella did not want to look at Mr. Merriman, lying across her aunt's beautiful mahogany table like an overfed pig dozing in its sty.

But she could not have seen him clearly even if she had tried as her eyes were blurred with stinging tears.

"So, Rosella," Lord Brockley went on. "You have no fortune, no family, no beau to take you off my hands, so you had better make yourself useful. Get that old fool out of my sight and take him to his room."

"But – "

Rosella's skin crawled at the thought of touching Algernon.

Lord Brockley slapped his hand on the table.

"Get to it!" he shouted. "And just remember whose house this is!"

Rosella jumped up and went around the table. She lifted one of Algernon's plump arms and he rolled his head and sighed, "brandy."

He did not open his eyes, even when she shook his arm and there was no way that she could move his heavy sleeping bulk.

"I can't – " she began, but before she could say any more, Mrs. Dawkins came into the dining room.

"The coffee, my Lord," she announced, placing a large silver pot on the table.

Then she saw Rosella.

"Oh, my Lady, you mustn't – "

Lord Brockley banged his hand on the table again.

"Get him out of here and into his bed," he shouted. "Or he will be good for nothing in the morning!"

Mrs. Dawkins scurried around the table and took Algernon's other arm.

Between the two of them, they managed to heave his heavy body onto its feet. Algernon lifted up his head and blinked a couple of times.

"Can you walk, sir?" the housekeeper asked him.

"No!" he spluttered, as his head fell forward again.

"Please try, if you can," Rosella suggested, as her shoulder was already aching with the weight of him.

"Oh, my angel!" he smiled woozily. "Hold on tight to me, that's the ticket."

At a snail's pace, Rosella and Mrs. Dawkins helped him to make his way to the door of the dining room and then across the hall.

It was very difficult, as he was most reluctant to take a step if he did not have to and he was much too heavy for them to carry.

"Just let me rest," he groaned, sitting down with a bump on the stairs. "And be with my little sweetheart."

Rosella felt his hand gripping her arm and trying to pull her down with him.

"No!" she cried, her voice catching in her throat. "You must go to your room. Get up."

He shook his head.

"Shan't!" he muttered in a childish voice.

"His Lordship will be exceedingly angry," Rosella whispered, glancing over her shoulder, as she half expected Lord Brockley to be watching their slow progress.

But there was no sign of him. He must be still at the table, sipping his coffee and finishing his cigar.

Her words had the desired effect, however, as, with much puffing and blowing, Algernon heaved himself onto his feet and stumbled up the stairs clinging to the banister with one hand and onto Rosella with the other.

Mrs. Dawkins brought up the rear, administering a shove to the small of his back whenever he looked as if he was coming to a halt.

When they reached his bedroom door, he gave out a loud groan, staggered in and tumbled onto the carpet.

"What shall we do?" Rosella asked, looking at Mrs. Dawkins, who was still catching her breath.

"Come to me, my sweetheart!" he gurgled, reaching out to catch hold of Rosella's skirts.

Mrs. Dawkins turned red with embarrassment.

"My Lady. Please, come away. You must not go into a gentleman's bedroom, it would not be proper."

"I don't want to," Rosella replied. "But we cannot just leave him there."

"I will send for one of the footmen or perhaps two of them to help him into bed," Mrs. Dawkins suggested. "Oh, Lady Rosella. What a night! I don't think I've ever seen two gentlemen eat and drink so much. Smoking those cigars at table. And now this! Will it always be the same from now on, do you think?"

"Let's hope not, Mrs. Dawkins," Rosella answered.

But deep inside herself, she knew that what she had seen tonight was just the beginning of her difficulties with Lord Brockley and Algernon Merriman.

*

A bright ray of sunlight, which had found its way through the thick curtain material and onto his narrow hard bed, woke Lyndon.

For a moment he had no idea where he was – even the dark clothes that were hanging over the iron rail at the end of the bed were unfamiliar.

He took a deep breath and smelt river water and tar, all mixed together with the tang of beer and frying bacon and then he remembered that he was staying at a small inn close to the London Docks.

The strange clothes, of course, were his disguise!

He looked at his watch, and saw that it was only half past five. He could curl up and sleep for at least another hour.

But then he recalled last night and his heart swelled with excruciating pain as he remembered the cold look on Marian's pretty face as she took the arm of his best friend and turned away from him.

He would never be able to rest properly with such thoughts surging through his mind.

Below the window of his little room, he could hear iron horseshoes slipping over the cobblestones and men's voices speaking in a strong Cockney accent.

He would get some breakfast from the innkeeper's wife and go out to see what was going on.

An hour later, he found himself by a great wharf, looking up at a forest of tall masts pointing at the sky.

The wharf was thronged with rough sailors dressed in grimy sea jackets and baggy trousers, men of all colours and nationalities, shouting and arguing with each other as they disembarked from the ships moored on the river.

There were Africans, Indians, a Chinaman carrying two baskets on a yoke and many Englishmen from London, Bristol and Liverpool, their faces burnt by tropical suns so that they were almost as dark as the Indians. All of them walked with a rolling gait as if they were still treading the decks of a wave-tossed ship.

No one took any notice of the mysterious black-cloaked figure in the wide hat.

'I could so easily slip on board one of these ships,' Lyndon thought, 'hide among the cargo and be carried off to anywhere. The Spice Islands, Australia, Brazil!'

One ship in particular caught his fancy. It was not one of the largest, but its sides were beautifully painted in black and gold.

He moved closer and saw that there was an unusual figurehead at the prow, a most shapely carved woman with a black mask covering her eyes.

And next to the figurehead, he read the words *La Maschera*.

It must be the name of the ship. There was another word painted on it, but he was too far away to make it out.

"*Scusi!*"

A dark sailor carrying a large trunk decorated with swirling patterns of leaves and flowers nudged him aside.

Lyndon apologised and moved out of the way.

The sailor then loaded the trunk onto the back of a coach that was waiting at the side of the wharf and then came jogging back towards the ship. He must be one of the crew.

"Your ship, where is she from? Lyndon asked him.

The man grinned, revealing several missing teeth.

"*La Maschera!*" he said proudly waving at the ship.

"Yes, yes. But where from?"

He pointed towards the wide river beyond the ship and looked questioningly at the sailor, whose black brows creased together and then suddenly he laughed,

"*Venezia!*"

"Of course! Venice." Lyndon said, remembering the Italian pronunciation of the famous City that seemed to rise up out of the water.

"*Si. Si! Venezia!*" the sailor now grinned even more broadly and, tapping his chest to indicate that he too came from that City. "*Anch'io Veneziano.*"

Now some sort of commotion seemed to be taking place on board and the sailor left Lyndon's side and stood by the gangplank that led from the deck to the wharf.

An old woman, dressed in black and with a gold-embroidered shawl wrapped around her head, had emerged from the cabin on the deck of *La Maschera*.

Lyndon caught his breath in surprise as a tiny imp-like creature wearing a red jacket and trousers and a small red hat suddenly leapt from the woman's shoulder and then bounded across the deck.

A high-pitched shriek issued from the old woman's lips and she raised her hands high in the air. Lyndon saw that in one of them she held a long black walking stick.

Now the whole deck was full of people – sailors, lady's maids, a cook with a big ladle in his hand, rushing everywhere and looking under piles of rope and luggage.

The red-jacketed imp was nowhere to be found and the woman's shrieks grew louder, so that all the hustle and bustle of the wharf came to a halt as people crowded round to see what was happening.

Lyndon was just pushing his way to the front of the crowd, when he felt an odd sensation around his right leg, as if someone was pulling at the hem of his trousers.

He looked down and to his great surprise he found himself gazing into a mournful pair of round dark eyes.

It was a small monkey, dressed in a red costume.

"So it is you, causing all the fuss," he whispered.

He reached down and the monkey caught his hand and then swung itself up, so that it was on his arm and it sat there, making a strange chattering noise.

Lyndon gazed at the tall masts of *La Maschera*, and thought how uncanny it was, that only a few moments ago he had seen this beautiful ship for the first time and now with the tiny monkey in his arms, he had the perfect excuse to go on board.

It was as if he was in the grip of something beyond his control, a strange irresistible force that was taking him over, drawing him to the ship and the distant mysterious City of Venice.

For a moment, Lyndon wanted to escape, to run away from this new world that was drawing him in like a magnet.

It was too late.

The little monkey clambered up onto his shoulder and wrapped its arm around his neck and a shout went up from the men who were standing beside him.

"'E's 'ere! The little blighter. The fella in black's got 'im!"

Lyndon next found himself being pushed forward towards the gangplank of the ship, where the rough hands of the sailor he had just spoken to pulled him on board.

The old woman in the black dress threw back the golden shawl from her grey head and gave a cry of joy.

A flood of passionate Italian words poured out from her, as the monkey leapt from his shoulder into her arms.

"*Caro mio! Piccolino Pepe, sei troppo cattivo!*" she cried and then she turned to Lyndon.

"*Grazie tanto, Signore,*" she said and then looked closely at him. "*Sei Italiano?*" she asked.

"No – I am English!" Lyndon replied, hoping that he had understood her correctly.

"Aaah. *Capisco.* I thought from your cloak and your hat – you were *Italiano.*"

She must be very old, Lyndon thought, for the curls that were piled up on her head were almost white, but her black eyes blazed with a fierce energy.

And she was clearly someone of great importance, as heavy gold rings gleamed on her fingers and her shawl was thick with swirls of gold thread.

"Who are you?" she asked. "What is your name?"

Lyndon was thrown into confusion. What should he say? Why had he not thought of a name for himself?

She asked again, her tone imperious and impatient. She was not someone who was used to being kept waiting.

"Mr. Jones," Lyndon now mumbled saying the very first name that came into his head.

"Oh – *Signore Jones!* How can I ever repay you for bringing back my naughty child?"

She caressed the monkey's little head and spoke to one of the mob-capped maids who stood beside her.

One maid took the creature and ran off.

"It was nothing, really," Lyndon said and he would

have turned to go, but the old woman touched his sleeve.

"This is my first time in England. And I am here for business matters and to see all the sights of your great City," she was now saying, struggling with the unfamiliar words. "*Signore* Jones, you must dine with me tonight!"

She reached into a small embroidered bag that hung at her waist and took out a white card and a gold pencil.

She scribbled something on the card and gave it to Lyndon.

Printed on the card, in gold letters he saw the words *La Contessa Allegrini*.

So the old woman was from the Italian Nobility – a Contessa! There was an address as well, *Ca' degli Angeli, Venezia*.

Beneath these words, the Contessa had written in a large sprawling hand, *The Palace Hotel, Bayswater.*

"Tonight! *Stasera*," she said. "I will give you the finest dinner in London. And you will tell me about your City, for I know nothing. I need a friend who will help me around and teach me your ways in England."

Lyndon hesitated.

He could not possibly go to the old woman's hotel and dine with her, as he would surely be spotted at once by someone who knew him and yet she was looking at him so fiercely that he did not dare say 'no' to her.

The Contessa laughed.

"Ah, you *inglesi*! I have heard about your famous shyness. Your silences, your lack of words. So different from we *italiani*!"

She tapped him on the arm.

"Until tonight, Mr. Jones."

And she then turned to the sailor who stood by the

gangplank and allowed him to help her onto dry land.

The crowd of onlookers parted respectfully as she walked towards the coach.

A hand gently touched Lyndon's arm. It was the maid who had gone into the cabin.

The monkey was safely on her shoulder and he saw that it now had a red ribbon tied around its waist, the other end of which was attached to the maid's wrist.

"*Signore*," she whispered and pressed a twist of paper into his hand. "*Grazie tanto.*"

And then she hurried away to join her Mistress.

Lyndon unfolded the paper to see, nestling inside, a handful of golden coins.

The Contessa had rewarded him well for rescuing her pet.

*

A sledgehammer was beating away at the inside of Algernon's head and, just to add to the pain, a whole army of birds were assaulting his delicate ears with loud shrieks and trills and warblings.

Where the hell was he? He groaned in agony and forced his heavy eyelids to open.

He closed them again quickly as, to his horror, the bedroom where he lay was flooded with brilliant sunlight. Why had his valet opened the curtains?

And then he remembered where he was. He had come down to Hampshire to be with Lord Brockley.

That was why the birds were being so noisy, he was in the middle of the countryside with trees and bushes all around instead of the bricks and stones of London.

It was simply impossible for him to sink back into the restful sleep that was the only cure for a headache such as the one that was threatening to split his skull open.

Why had he thought it such a good idea to come to the country?

Reluctantly, Algernon opened his tired eyes and sat up, clutching his forehead in his hands.

Now he noticed that the same useless servant who had opened up the curtains and who clearly did not know about his preference for late rising had left a tray of tea and toast on the small table beside his bed.

Tea. Perhaps that would help to clear his throbbing head. He reached for the teapot, but it was quite cold.

He must have slept very late indeed this morning. Lord Brockley, who never seemed to suffer quite so badly from the after-effects of over-indulgence in brandy, would be waiting for him.

Algernon gave another groan and heaved his legs over the side of the bed.

There was a full jug of water on the washstand and he staggered over to it and poured himself a glass.

Then, feeling just a little better, he went over to the window to draw the curtains against the frightful glare and to shut out the awful noise the birds were making.

Outside a soft breeze was stirring the tops of the tall trees that surrounded the gardens below his window.

He was just about the tug the heavy curtain closed, when something caught his eye – a flash of gold, moving among the flowers.

It was the pretty girl who had sat opposite him at dinner last night, the little angel who he could swear had brought him luck in the dice game at the inn.

She was down there in the Rose Garden, a basket over her arm, cutting blooms.

She moved so prettily in her violet-coloured dress

and he saw that her long golden curls reached almost to her slender waist.

He noticed the sunlight gleaming on her curls and remembered how the soft candlelight last night had shone on them, making a pale halo around her sweet young face.

She had been so shy and quiet all through dinner, as if she did not want to attract any attention to herself.

Algernon normally preferred lively and flirtatious girls, like the delicious dark-haired creature, who had been engaged to Lord Brockley's son – nothing reticent about her at all!

But there was indeed something about the shyness and reserve of this girl, Rosella, that was very enticing.

As he watched her reach up to cut a white rose from a tall branch, he suddenly thought how delightful it would be to slip his arm around her waist and draw her to him.

And the touch of one of her soft little hands on his forehead would completely cure his headache.

He had no memory of being helped from the dining room last night and almost carried up the stairs by Rosella and Mrs. Dawkins.

Nor did he recall the expression of revulsion on Rosella's pretty face as she looked down at him where he lay on his bedroom carpet.

For he was never able to remember anything that happened to him when he had taken too much brandy.

There was a loud rap at his bedroom door and then it flew open.

"Get up!" Lord Brockley growled as he strode over the carpet. "Luncheon will be served in a few moments."

He scowled at Algernon still in his nightshirt.

"What have you been doing all morning? I want to

place a bet on the big race this afternoon and I should like your opinion on the runners."

"I'm almost up, Carlton. I was just admiring the wonderful view of the gardens."

Lord Brockley came to join him at the window.

"Ah! I might have guessed," he said.

And, as he too looked down on Rosella, making her way through the Rose Garden, a thoughtful expression came over his face.

# CHAPTER FIVE

"Thomas – wait," Rosella called out, as she saw the gardener's boy hurrying down the drive through the misty summer rain.

"My Lady?"

Thomas stopped in his tracks and turned to face her, raindrops clinging to his thatch of fair hair.

"I have not seen you for so long," Rosella said. "Is everything all right with you?"

Thomas hesitated a moment before he replied,

"Yes, it is, my Lady."

"Where are you off to in such a hurry?"

"I am going to the bookmakers to place a bet for his Lordship."

"But surely that is not your job, Thomas."

Thomas looked uncomfortable.

"Well, my Lady. Things 'ave changed 'ere. I don't spend so much time in the garden. I have other duties. The gentlemen are always findin' things for me to do."

Rosella sighed.

That would explain why there were so many weeds pushing up through the path that wound through the Rose Garden and why dead heads still clung to the bushes.

"My Lady, you should not be out in this weather, you'll get soaked," Thomas remarked.

Rosella could feel cold water leaking through the sole of her right shoe and big drops were sliding from the edge of her umbrella and splashing onto the grass.

"You are right, Thomas. I suppose I had better go in and you must go on your errand."

She watched him walk away down the drive and wondered why Lord Brockley had not thought to order the pony and trap for Thomas, for it was several miles into Winchester.

Or why, indeed, he had not sent his friend Mr. Merriman to run the errand.

Mr. Algernon Merriman, who, at this very moment, was lounging languidly on the sofa in the drawing room, doing absolutely nothing except to recover from too many helpings of roast beef and gooseberry pie at luncheon.

She had seen him there every afternoon for the last week, sipping brandy – 'for my digestion' as he liked to say and reading the newspaper.

If Rosella was there, he would ask her to read to him. She had never known a man so lazy – or so greedy.

Even Lord Brockley seemed somewhat impatient and exasperated with the slothfulness of his companion.

But in truth, Rosella reckoned, she preferred Mr. Merriman like this.

For sometimes, when he saw her, he would rouse himself and become full of energy and enthusiasm, which was very unpleasant.

This was the reason that Rosella was out in the Park now despite the rain, as she simply could not bear to be in the same room as Algernon.

Over the last week he had followed her everywhere, calling her endlessly 'my little angel' and constantly trying to kiss her hand.

She shivered at the memory of his plump fingers against hers and then the wind shook the tree above her and icy drops slid down her umbrella, soaking her dress.

The rain was falling more heavily now and Rosella was getting very cold from standing around so long in it.

Perhaps if she was very quiet, she might be able to creep into New Hall by the back door and escape to her bedroom without anyone noticing her.

At first her plan seemed to be working. Rosella slipped through the back door and was just about to go up the narrow back staircase, which was usually only used by the servants, when Mrs. Dawkins came out of the kitchen.

"My Lady!" she called. "Thank goodness. You're wanted in the study."

Rosella's heart sank. The study! So Lord Brockley wishes to speak to her.

What could he possibly have to say? She had kept out of his way all week and, although she had caught him watching her sometimes with his hooded eyes, he had not made any further remarks to her about her fortune or the necessity of her finding a husband.

She had kept Pickle out of earshot in her bedroom and she had been quiet and respectful at table, despite the rude and unpleasant behaviour of him and his companion.

Every evening after dinner she and Mrs. Dawkins had helped the drunk and helpless Algernon safely to his bedroom door.

Surely there could be nothing for Lord Brockley to criticise in her behaviour.

"Does he look – angry, Mrs. Dawkins?" she asked.

"For once, he seems quite cheerful," Mrs. Dawkins replied with a little sigh.

Several new lines had suddenly appeared on the

housekeeper's face, giving her an anxious tired appearance.

"But you must not keep him waiting any longer – I have been looking for you for ages."

Rosella handed Mrs. Dawkins her wet umbrella and made her way to the study.

"Come in!" Lord Brockley's deep voice growled, as she tapped on the door.

She stepped inside, her heart beating fast and stood on the carpet in front of him.

"Good afternoon, sir," she began, her voice a little shaky, as it always was when she had to speak to him.

"I am very pleased," he said, after a long pause, "to have found a solution to two difficulties which have been bothering me this last week."

His hooded eyes gleamed at her through the fog of cigar smoke that always surrounded him.

"I am sorry, sir. I don't understand," Rosella said, holding herself as straight as she could, as her knees felt very weak.

"*You* are one of my difficulties, Rosella. You have no fortune. No place to go. And – if you stay here in this house, an unmarried girl of good family, there will be talk – scandal even."

Rosella's skin prickled with unease.

Lord Brockley was still talking,

"I don't much care what people think, but I could do without the fuss and bother of it all."

"I would not dream of causing any – trouble – " she stammered.

"I should hope not," Lord Brockley replied. "I have been watching you. You are a good girl. You rise early, you don't over-indulge at table and you do everything you are asked to do, you are happy to be seen and not heard."

"Thank you, sir."

"But you are still a problem for me. I am plagued with so much indolence, intemperance and unpunctuality. Unecessary irritations preventing me from enjoying myself while I am here at New Hall. I think you could help me to stop all this. Would you do that, Rosella?"

"Of course, sir," Rosella replied, although she was not at all sure what he meant.

"Excellent." he smiled benignly. "Then surely your own good qualities of industry, restraint and punctuality will cure these irritations. Is that not common sense?"

"I – suppose so, sir."

"You would like to stay here at New Hall, would you not?"

"Oh, yes!" Rosella's heart gave a great leap of joy.

"Of course you would."

Lord Brockley stood up and pulled the tasselled cord that hung by the fireplace.

A young parlourmaid came to the door.

"Tell Mr. Merriman I want him," he said, "you will find him, no doubt, half asleep in the drawing room."

The parlourmaid bobbed a curtsy and hurried off.

"May I go now, sir?" Rosella asked.

"No! You may not leave. I don't think you have understood. If my solution to the problem is to be carried out, it is absolutely necessary that you stay."

Lord Brockley gave short bark of laughter and went to the door.

"Ah – Merriman!" he greeted his friend, who was just about to come in. "She has agreed. I shall leave you to it!"

And with that Lord Brockley left the study.

*

It was getting dark and the wharf was quiet now – the sailors were either resting on board or enjoying a night off in one of the many inns and taverns around the docks.

Lyndon walked slowly along by the river, keeping to the shadows.

He did not want anyone from *La Maschera* to recognise him. But the beautiful ship was silent and no lights shone, just one lantern at the masthead.

He gazed up at the figurehead, the lovely carved woman with the jewelled mask over her eyes.

In the twilight she looked even more mysterious than before, as the rays from the ship's lantern cast alluring shadows over her face and glinted on the mask.

Who was she? Someone real or a character from a story?

Lyndon closed his eyes and pictured row upon row of old buildings, their painted and gilded shutters reflected in the dark waters of the canals that flowed beneath them.

The Palazzos of Venice – he had seen so many paintings of them and now he longed to see them for real and see too the famous masked balls he had read about.

Maybe in Venice there were a great many beautiful masked women just like the voluptuous figurehead.

He could dance with these masked beauties, hold them in his arms, perhaps even kiss one of them and he would never have to know who they were and never have to give them his heart, as he had done to Marian.

He had felt afraid at first of the strange magnetism that seemed to be drawing him to the City that rose like a mirage out of the Venetian lagoon.

But tonight he felt braver. Why should he not give in to this mysterious attraction?

He left the silent *La Maschera* and headed back to the crowded bar of the inn where he was staying.

The sailors who came regularly to drink rum at the inn had grown used to the frequent comings-and-goings of the mysterious black-cloaked man and they shouted out to him to come and join them.

"Don't be a stranger!" one man yelled. "Sit down, take the weight of your feet. I'll stand you a pint of ale."

Lyndon squeezed himself onto the wooden bench next to the man.

The ale, when it arrived, was dark in colour and tasted very strong, but he found that he quite liked it.

And it felt very good to be in the company of these friendly sailors, who seemed to want nothing from him but that he should enjoy himself.

He had drunk two pints of the ale and was feeling rather merry, when the brawny man leaned over and said,

"You're a good fellow, sir, there's no doubt. But you're a man of mystery! What brings you here and why do you stay among us? What is your business?"

Lyndon felt suddenly reckless.

"I am seeking a passage to Venice," he replied.

"Ah," the man sighed. "Venice! The most beautiful City I ever saw."

Another sailor, a thin man sporting a gold earring, leaned across the table.

"We're bound for Venice. We sail on the evening tide in three days' time," he declared in a Scottish accent.

Lyndon fumbled in one of the pockets of his cloak and pulled out a couple of the gold coins the Contessa had given him.

"Here," he said. "I'll come with you, if I may!"

The thin sailor's eyes widened as he saw the gold and he scooped up the coins at once.

The brawny man laughed.

"Good job your cloak is black, sir. For it be coal they be a-carryin'!"

Now Lyndon saw that there were smears of black dust on the face of the sailor with the gold earring, but he did not mind having to share the voyage with such a cargo.

Now he had made the decision, his heart felt light and his veins sang with anticipation.

"It be *The Grace Darling*," the brawny man said. "You'll find her down at the end of the wharf."

He turned to the other man.

"Now, Jock! Don't you go runnin' off with that gold! Mind you go and tell the Captain you'll be carryin' a passenger. And that he's paid you a more than fair price for the voyage."

The sailor grinned and reached across the table and shook Lyndon's hand.

"Come by *The Grace Darling* tomorrow and speak to the Captain yourself," he suggested. "He'll be right glad to take you."

And Lyndon, his head swimming with ale and with the cloudy vision of Venice rising up out of the water, got up from the table and stumbled up the stairs to his room.

He did not know how he was going to get through the next three days, as he simply could not wait to be on his way.

*

Algernon Merriman had put on weight in the last week, Rosella thought, as the buttons on his waistcoat were straining to burst open.

But he seemed rather more sprightly than usual, as he paced up and down, rubbing his plump hands together.

"Well, well, my little angel," he called, his small eyes gleaming. "This is a very happy day!"

"Good afternoon, sir," Rosella said politely. "I am glad you are feeling so cheerful."

For a moment she wondered if he had won some money at cards or had placed a lucky bet.

Algernon nodded eagerly.

"Oh yes. I have seldom felt more joyful than I did just now, when his Lordship told me that you would be agreeable to his plan!"

"Of course I must always respect his Lordship's wishes," Rosella replied slowly. "But – "

"Then you might look just a little more pleased," he exclaimed. "It's not every day a girl like yourself with no prospects and such a shy violet as you are too gets a chance like this!"

He seized Rosella's hand in his, pushing his face up close to hers.

She looked down to avoid his eyes that were gazing at her in a way that made her feel really uncomfortable and noticed there was egg stain on his bulging silk waistcoat.

"I don't know what you mean, sir," she said, trying to free her hand.

"You are going to be my wife, young lady! His Lordship's suggestion and one which – I must say – I find utterly delightful!"

He crushed her hand against his lips and called her his little angel several times in a breathless passionate tone that made Rosella's skin crawl.

"But I could not – "

She tried once again to escape from him.

"Ah, ha!" Algernon rolled his eyes upwards. "You divine little thing. You are so modest, so exquisitely shy, that you make me want you more than any other girl I've ever seen."

She managed at last to snatch her hand out of his.

"I do *not* wish to marry you," she asserted. "I did not understand what Lord Brockley meant – I could never marry you!"

Algernon pursed his lips and shook his head at her in a childish teasing manner.

"But Lady Rosella, how can you refuse? We have been brought together by the Fates, it is quite clear."

"I don't think so!"

She longed to run out of the study, but Algernon's considerable bulk was between her and the door.

"Of course, you are not the type of young lady that I would normally pursue, for you are certainly very retiring and somewhat backward in putting yourself forward I must say," he was braying, his greedy eyes fixed on her face.

"But, from the first moment I saw you, with your pretty hair shining in the sunlight and your lovely little figure, so neat and so trim, I knew that you were my lucky angel. Why, it was because of you I won that fifty pounds at cards."

"How could that be?" Rosella said, "I know nothing about cards. I was simply looking for my carriage."

And then her heart turned over as she remembered what Lord Brockley had said – for how much longer could she call New Hall her home?

Algernon lunged forward and, as Rosella stepped back to move away from him, he grabbed hold of her skirts and pulled her against him.

"Oh, my darling!" he gasped. "You must be mine. How can I live without you."

"No," Rosella cried, feeling she would suffocate if she did not get away from him.

"Yes! Yes!"

He then buried his face in her shoulder and kissed it passionately.

"I need you. You must be my wife and take care of me, my darling angel."

Now at last Rosella understood what Lord Brockley had meant when he spoke to her a few moments ago.

He intended her to marry Mr. Algernon Merriman and keep him out of trouble.

He wanted her to stop his companion from getting too drunk and behaving foolishly and to make sure that he got up in the morning, ready to join in whatever activities his Lordship had planned for the day.

And then – only then – would she be able to stay on at New Hall, her beloved home.

Her heart felt as if it would burst.

How could she possibly marry this man? She could not bear him, the sound of his childish voice, the touch of his hot plump hands. There was nothing about him that she could possibly like.

With a great effort she dragged her skirts out of his grasp and ran to the door.

"Come back, my angel," he called out.

Rosella shut the door in his face and ran upstairs to her bedroom.

She sat on her bed and buried her face in her hands and her tears fell as fast as the rain that dripped from the gutters outside her window.

"*Are you all right, my dear?*" a small voice asked.

She looked up and could see through her tears that Pickle was watching her from his cage.

He might only be a bird, but he seemed to know exactly how she was feeling.

"What shall I do?" she asked him. "I don't like Mr. Merriman at all – but do you think I should marry him, so that we can – stay here?"

But Pickle did not have the answer to her question.

He just put his head on one side and enquired,

"*Is it time for tea?*"

Rosella had not been in her bedroom for more than half an hour, when she heard heavy footfalls on the landing outside.

Her heart turned over as an angry fist beat loudly on the panels of her door and then it flew open and Lord Brockley strode towards her, his face flushed with rage.

"Insolent, stupid girl!" he shouted. "What do you mean by refusing Merriman! You agreed that you would obey my wishes."

Pickle squealed loudly and fluffed up his feathers.

"*Stop it at once, you naughty boy!*" he squawked.

Lord Brockley's faced turned an even darker shade of red.

"Quiet, you little devil!" he screamed back.

"I did not understand what you meant when we spoke," Rosella said, and although she was trembling, her words came out clear and strong.

Lord Brockley's lips parted in an angry snarl.

"Let me show you what I mean. *Merriman!*"

Algernon then appeared in the doorway, looking flustered and foolish.

"Show me what you are made of," his Lordship called out, glaring at him. "Be a man!"

Algernon stepped forward into the room.

"Rosella," he quavered, his voice coming out in a squeak. "You must be my wife."

Lord Brockley grabbed him by the shoulder and shook him.

"*Be a man!*" he shouted. "She's just a foolish girl – make her accept you or it will be the worse for you both."

"No!"

Feeling terrified, Rosella ran to the window, where Pickle's cage stood. He was flapping his wings in fear.

"Marry me!" Algernon whined, following her over the room. "You and I – we'll get along very well here at New Hall, won't we? And I adore you. How many times must I keep telling you?"

"I can't!" Rosella cried. "I don't want to marry you. I will never marry you!"

In desperation she looked out of the window.

It was a long drop to the lead roof of the orangery, which lay below, gleaming wet under the heavy rain.

Lord Brockley pushed Algernon to one side and came over to face Rosella.

"I'm warning you, if you don't do as I wish, you will be very sorry indeed," he yelled.

"*Stop it, stop it, stop it! Be quiet!*" Pickle screamed, his voice even louder than Lord Brockley's.

His Lordship gave a roar of anger and, seizing the cage, he forced open the window and threw it out.

There was a crash, as the cage hit the top of the orangery and smashed in two.

Pickle gave a shriek of fear, then climbed out from

his broken cage and flew away into the rain, disappearing into the trees.

"Oh, no," Rosella cried. "Come back, Pickle!"

But the bird was gone.

Lord Brockley slammed the window shut.

"Good riddance," he grunted.

He took Rosella's arm in a painful grip.

"There will be *no* further nonsense from you," he said, his tone cold and hard. "You will stay here in your bedroom and you will have no dinner, no luncheon and no breakfast until you come to your senses."

He turned to Algernon,

"And you, sir, will go on repeating your proposal until it is accepted."

Rosella was shivering with fear and shock and her voice, which had seemed so strong a few moments ago, seemed to have deserted her.

Lord Brockley gave her arm a final agonising twist with his strong hand and then, pushing Algernon in front of him, he left Rosella's bedroom and she heard the ominous click of a key in the lock.

Shaking, she sat down on her bed.

Rosella now felt utterly alone and yet she suddenly found herself whispering,

"Help me, please, please. Help me!"

She thought longingly of Aunt Beatrice. She had missed her terribly, but never so much as at this moment.

And for the first time in a long while, she missed her Mama and her Papa, whom she had so few memories of, only their loving voices and the embrace of their arms.

She clung onto herself desperately.

If only there was someone in the world to hold her,

to care for her and speak gentle kind words –

Suddenly she felt that someone was watching her, and she looked up to see the portrait of the young man in the turban hanging on the wall above her.

"Why are you smiling?" she asked him. "Look at me. I am in such despair!"

Her tears welled up in her eyes once again, but then she realised that his smile was not mocking but bold and happy.

His bright dark eyes seemed to be comforting and encouraging her.

"*I* care for you – " he was almost saying.

Then Rosella remembered all the times that she had fallen down and hurt herself as a child.

Aunt Beatrice had always picked her up, comforted her and smiled in a bright and encouraging way, so that she would quickly feel much better and carry on playing.

She gave a last great sob and stopped crying.

'That is what I must do,' she whispered to herself. 'I must pick myself up and keep going.'

For dear Aunt Beatrice had left her something that might help her, if only she could escape.

Rosella went to her dressing table and checked that the silver mesh bag with the coins inside was still there.

Then she went to the window.

Lord Brockley had not locked it and, if she used her sheets and bedcovers, she would be able to let herself down onto the orangery roof.

And surely from there it would be possible to jump down to the ground.

But then she would have to wait until everyone was asleep.

# CHAPTER SIX

The rain fell all through the long afternoon and it was still pattering against the windows and splashing down the gutters when Algernon came to Rosella's room again.

This time he was not in such a sprightly mood as when he had first proposed to her in the study.

"You had better say you will marry me," he said in a petulant tone, "or you will have no dinner."

"I cannot," she replied and took hold of the chair that stood by her dressing table and held it between them, so that he could not come near her.

Algernon shook his head.

"It's the best offer you will ever get – seeing as you have no fortune and no prospects. And there's a delicious roast goose for dinner!"

Rosella thought that she would be sick if she had to even look at the rich greasy meat of roast goose, let alone eat it.

"Don't be a silly girl," Algernon was saying. "I've been in love with so many pretty young things and none of them have I asked to become Mrs. Merriman! Just think of that. Doesn't it make you feel proud?"

He then smiled at Rosella and twirled the end of his moustache with a plump finger. She gave a deep shudder of revulsion, she could not help it.

He saw the shudder and his round face creased into a scowl.

"There's no need to look like that. You should be counting your blessings, young lady, and being very nice to someone who only has your best interests at heart."

Rosella gripped the back of the chair tightly. He was coming towards her now.

"Perhaps you are not such a sweet little thing after all," he asserted. "Perhaps I shall have to try a different approach to bring you to heel!"

In the next instant he had pulled the chair out of her hands and thrown it aside.

He grabbed Rosella's waist and there was a crash of silver-topped bottles falling over as he flung her against the dressing table mirror.

"Oh, how divine!" he grunted, pressing his heavy body against her.

She felt his hot breath on her face and then, to her horror, his hot lips fumbling at her cheek, trying to find her mouth.

"How delicious you are, you wilful little creature," he sighed.

Now he was touching her hair and her face with his thick fingers.

"You are so soft, my little angel," he whispered, his moustache scratching her ear. "Let Algernon adore you, that's the way."

Terror rose up in Rosella's chest. She could feel the burning tide of it pushing up through her body, as he pressed himself ever more closely against her, forcing the breath from her lungs.

"*Please*," she managed to gasp, closing her eyes so that she could no longer see his face.

She felt his bulky body shake with laughter.

"Please? Now that's more like it! What is it that you want from your Algernon, my pretty angel!"

"Let me go!"

"Of course, of course," he crooned. "But first you will kiss me and then you will promise to be my wife."

The tide of terror was threatening to overcome her and she realised that she was about to faint, for the same strange giddiness was now coming over her that she had experienced in the dressmaker's shop.

But she could not lose herself and lie helpless in the arms of Mr. Merriman.

With a huge effort she now opened her eyes wide, willing herself to stay conscious.

Over Algernon's shoulder, she saw that the young man in her painting was looking down at her with the same mischievous smile still on his face.

As her desperate gaze met his painted eyes, she felt strength and courage flooding back into her veins.

'*Help me, please!*' she prayed to him silently.

And then suddenly she heard music playing, violins and flutes and saw shadowy figures dancing under the light of a huge chandelier.

The young man stood in front of her, holding out his hands, his dark eyes glowing under the colourful turban that wreathed his head.

"What shall I do?" she asked him.

The young man laughed.

"*Outwit him!*" he replied. "*Play with him. He's a fool and you are far cleverer than he. Then you must dance with me – I have been waiting for you a very long time –* "

A wave of bliss rose up in her heart and she stood on tiptoe with the joy of the music and the thought that in just a moment she would be spinning across the floor of the great ballroom –

"Rosella! Lady Rosella?" Algernon's voice rang faintly in her ears and she felt his fingers against her cheek.

And then she was back in her bedroom, still pinned against her dressing table.

Her captor was frowning down at her.

"You have gone all pale and cold," he said. "I hope you are not going to be ill."

"I am fine," Rosella managed to say and she turned her head aside to buy a moment's time.

'*Outwit him*,' the young man had told her. But how could she do it?

"Good, I am waiting for a kiss," Algernon said in a childish wheedling tone. "And I shall not let you go until you have said you will be my wife."

"You are crushing me," Rosella cried. "Please, I can hardly speak."

"A kiss!" he demanded.

"I cannot breathe."

He shifted his weight a little, so that he did not lie so heavily on her, but kept his face close to hers.

"Come on, my little angel! A kiss."

"You ask a – lot of me."

"A kiss? Such a tiny thing."

His breath smelled of wine and beef from luncheon.

"A kiss is not – such a small thing for a girl like myself," Rosella countered.

She seemed to see the young man still smiling and nodding encouragement as she thought of what to say next.

"I – am very young – " she continued.

"And so sweet!"

Algernon squeezed her waist.

"I have never kissed anyone before."

"Then I shall be the first."

Algernon gave a little groan of delight.

"Indeed. But – dear Mr. Merriman, I cannot even think of such a thing until we are engaged."

"Oh," he said and a wide smile dawned on his face. "Then – you will do it. You will be Mrs. Merriman!"

"I will think about it," Rosella said. "I promise you that – I will think about it."

His smile faded a little.

"But – "

"It has all been so sudden," she went on, forcing herself to smile at him. "I have never had a proposal of marriage before. I must have time to get used to the idea."

"Do you know what you are asking me, you wicked girl?" he interrupted. "Have you any idea what agony it is to want you so much?"

"I know how much you care for me," Rosella said, lowering her eyelashes modestly. "Please, just a little time, is all I ask and then – "

"And then, believe me, I shall take all the kisses I want!"

Algernon sounded disgruntled, but, at long last, he released his grip on her waist.

Rosella then smoothed her skirts, trying to keep her trembling hands steady.

"So, I would suppose that now we have reached an agreement, I might allow you to come down and join us at dinner," Algernon smirked with a tweak of his moustache.

Rosella shook her head.

She could face neither the hot roast goose nor Lord Brockley, as she was sure that his Lordship would have no time for her little ruse and would see right through her.

He would insist that she gave a definite answer immediately.

"I am not at all hungry," she said. "I would like to stay here and think about your proposal, Mr. Merriman."

"You will say 'yes', won't you?" he said, turning back to look at her as he was about to leave her. "Of course you will! I shall tell his Lordship the good news."

And then, at long last, he was gone.

Rosella sat down on the end of her bed, shaking from head to foot.

Outside the rain still fell in sheets and it would not be dark for several hours.

She must prepare herself for what she had to do, and then she must wait until the conditions were absolutely perfect for her escape.

*

It was not till the early hours of the morning, when the sun was about to rise and the Park was full of soft grey light, that the rain stopped.

Many times through the night Rosella had almost climbed out through the window and let herself down onto the orangery roof.

But she was afraid of slipping on the wet tiles and a little afraid too of the dark as there was no moon.

But now she had to go.

The purse of sovereigns was tied onto a belt at her waist and hidden under her skirts.

In a small carpet bag, she had packed a couple of her dark blue cotton dresses and a few essential items.

She would have so loved to take the portrait of the young man in the turban, but it was too big and awkward for her to carry.

"Goodbye," she nodded to him, as she stood by the open window. "I will never forget how you have helped me tonight."

His eyes seemed to move a little in the dim early morning light, as if he heard her words and was wishing her well on her journey.

"*Be brave, Rosella,*" he seemed to say. "*All will be well.*"

She did not feel very brave, as she tossed her carpet bag out of the window and then, clinging onto the rope she had made by plaiting her bedcovers together, she lowered herself down onto the orangery roof, next to the smashed remains of Pickle's cage.

From the distant trees in the Park, a few birds were tuning up, beginning their dawn chorus.

With a pang in her heart, she thought of Pickle and wondered where he was and how he was faring out there in the wild.

All through the night, as the rain fell, he had been on her mind. He was not used to such conditions, having spent most of his life indoors.

But then she remembered that once he had been a wild bird and had lived in a tropical forest where rain fell almost all the time.

Perhaps he was glad to be free again, at last.

And she, Rosella, was free too.

For, now that she was embarked on her escape, it was relatively easy to clamber down the drainpipe at the side of the orangery.

Now she must go to Winchester, through the Park and over the wet farmland, staying away from the roads in case anyone should see her.

She was just setting off under the trees that grew at the side of the drive, when she heard a call that turned her veins to ice.

"Lady Rosella. Lady Rosella."

Someone was coming after her!

Too afraid to turn around, Rosella waited.

She heard footsteps running through the wet grass and then a hand touched her shoulder.

"Lady Rosella?" a soft Hampshire voice said.

It was Thomas, the gardener's boy.

"Oh, Thomas!"

Tears of relief sprang into Rosella's eyes.

"Please, be quiet. No one must know I am here."

She explained, the words spilling over themselves in her haste, that she must leave New Hall at once or marry Mr. Merriman.

Thomas's eyes were round with amazement.

"But Lady Rosella, you must not."

"No, Thomas. I cannot marry him. But I have to leave and secretly or they will come and force me to go back. They – they locked me in my room."

"My Lady, wait, and I'll go with you, I have to take some of the fruit from the garden into Winchester for the market and that's why I'm up so early. No one'll see us, they're all still a-bed."

"Thomas, you will get into trouble."

The boy shook his head.

"I'll find an old coat for you in the stables and a basket of eggs. If anyone sees us, they'll think you're one of the girls who works in the dairy goin' to market."

Rosella was so overcome at his kindness that she almost forgot herself and would have given him a hug.

But something flapped in the leaves over her head, sending sharp drops of water showering on her.

She blinked the water out of her eyes and peered upwards.

"*Hello*! *How are you*?" a small voice spoke up and the leaves rustled as a shadowy form fluttered down from the branches to land on her shoulder.

"It be Lady Beatrice's bird!" Thomas cried.

Pickle was looking rather wet and bedraggled, but his eyes were bright as he gazed affectionately at Rosella.

"Oh, Pickle! I am so glad you are all right," she whispered. "But whatever am I going to do with you? I cannot take you with me."

"*May I have a nut*?" Pickle asked, in his most polite voice. He did not seem to appreciate the seriousness of the situation.

"My Lady – there's an old birdcage at the stables. I saw it when we were sweepin' out the loft over the harness room," Thomas said. "The gardener told me it belonged to the little parakeet that her Ladyship had before she bought the parrot. I think he'd fit in it."

"Oh, Thomas, I don't know. How will I carry it?"

"It's not as big as his usual cage, my Lady. And – it can rest in my wheelbarrow on top of the fruit as we go to Winchester. Wait here."

He ran off, his feet sinking into the wet grass.

Pickle nodded his head as if in approval.

*"Chop, chop, hurry along there!"* he muttered to himself, sounding just like Mrs. Dawkins speaking to one of the maids.

Rosella laughed at him.

She felt very touched that he had chosen of his own free will to come down out of the tree to her. How could she think of leaving him behind, however hard it might be?

She scratched the feathers on top of his head and watched for Thomas to return and he soon came hurrying back with a laden wheelbarrow.

She wrapped the old coat that he had brought round her shoulders and took a last look at the beautiful frontage of New Hall.

The moment had come when she must say goodbye to her old home forever.

"Will you be all right, my Lady?" Thomas asked her, as they stood together on the platform at Winchester Station to wait for the London train.

"Of course I will." Rosella forced herself to sound bright and cheerful. "You must go back, Thomas, or they will wonder where you are."

"But my Lady – what will you do in London?"

"Oh, I have a little money. I shall be fine."

Rosella tried not to worry about the unknown City, crowded with strangers that waited for her at the end of the train journey.

"Do you have a place to go to?"

"No, but I – shall find some lodgings. And then, I will look for some kind of work – "

With every word she spoke, she felt more doubtful and afraid.

Thomas now asked if she had a pencil and paper.

"My sister lives at Limehouse, my Lady," he said. "In the East End of London. It's a poor enough place, just a sailor's cottage, but Sarah's a kind soul and, if she knows I sent you, she'll make you very welcome."

He wrote down in large clumsy letters the number of the house and the name of the street.

"Thank you so so much, Thomas."

Rosella did not dare to say any more, as she would break down into tears.

"Keep the old cloak on, my Lady, in case there be anyone on the train who might recognise you."

Rosella nodded and checked that Pickle's cage was well hidden from view under the old blanket that Thomas had given her.

"And, my Lady – "

Thomas's kind face was very pink as he took her hand to bid her farewell.

"Will you – will you write to me sometime, just to let me know you are safe? I'm no great one for readin' and writin', but a few short words will set my heart at rest. Just sign your letter *a friend* – and I'll know it's you."

Rosella nodded again and then with a shrill whistle, the train pulled slowly into the platform and she lost sight of Thomas in a cloud of steam.

"It is just you and I now, Pickle," she whispered, as she stepped into a Second Class carriage, her heart beating with apprehension.

But he did not reply, for, as always happened when a cover was put over his cage, he thought it was night-time and had fallen asleep.

*

"There's a couple of hours yet before the tide is at full flow," the Captain said in his precise Scottish accent.

"Take a turn about the wharf, young man, and stretch your legs. It'll be a few days before you get the chance again."

Lyndon would have preferred to go to his tiny cabin on board *The Grace Darling* and wait quietly there until the ship cast off.

London meant nothing to him now, his heart and soul were flying on ahead to Venice and he would not be happy until the voyage was begun.

He left his bags for one of the sailors to stow safely away and stepped back onto dry land.

It was now a quiet time by the river. The afternoon bustle had ended and it would be a little while before the nightly crowd of revellers came down to fill the inns and taverns with their shouts and laughter.

The sun had not quite set and the twilight sky was full of purple and lavender, reflecting its deep colours onto the silvery surface of the Thames.

'How much more beautiful it will be in Venice,' Lyndon thought, remembering the paintings he had seen, 'where there is water everywhere and the sky seems so much wider.'

His mind was so far away that he barely noticed that there was someone standing, all alone, by the side of the river, until he tripped over a strangely-shaped bundle beside this person and almost fell flat on his face.

There was a loud shriek and an odd creaky little voice warbled,

"*Mind how you go – please!*"

Lyndon looked around, expecting to see that the voice had come from an old woman who owned the parcel.

Instead, he found himself staring into a pair of deep blue eyes, belonging to a girl so pretty she seemed to have come from another world altogether than this dark dingy wharf.

85

Her skin was white and her hair a bright shining gold, surrounding her lovely face like the halo of an angel in a painting.

Lyndon was so shocked by the sight of her that he completely forgot his manners.

"Who?  What – ?" he stammered.

"*Hello*!" the odd croaking voice spoke again, but the girl's lips did not move.

"I am sorry," he said, now completely mystified.  "I didn't see you there and I tripped."

"It's my fault," the girl replied and her soft voice echoed in his ears and sent shivers down his spine, as it felt as if he must have heard it before somewhere very dear to him and yet he could not quite remember.

"I came down to the river to get some air, for the house where I am staying is very cramped and I thought I would bring Pickle too."

"Pickle?"

Lyndon looked down and saw that the bundle at her feet was a round birdcage with a blanket tied around it.

Inside it was a large grey parrot, which was eyeing him suspiciously with its bright intelligent eye.

"Oh, good evening, Pickle," he said.  "Now at last I understand."

The bird stared at him disapprovingly.

"He is rather shy with strangers," the girl explained.

Lyndon raised his eyes to her face again.

She spoke clearly and sweetly with no trace of any accent.

Her skin was fine and soft and the hand with which she held her old coat together at the collar was slender and delicate.  She was not at all like the rough girls and women who frequented the docks, especially in the late evening.

"We have not been introduced," Lyndon said shyly.

Surely, this girl must be of good birth, if not noble birth. Yet he had not seen her before at any of the London parties and *soirées* he had attended.

"My name is – Mr. Jones."

"And I am – Jane," she answered, gravely. "I am staying here with my friend, Sarah, while I look for work."

"Work?" he asked, forgetting his manners again, as he could not imagine this lovely girl serving ale in a tavern or sewing seams in the back room of a dress-shop.

She turned a little pink, as if she was embarrassed and he quickly pulled himself together.

"And how is your search going?" he asked her in a polite tone.

"Oh, I have had several offers," she replied with a little sigh. "There are plenty of posts for Governesses and companions."

"That's good!"

"But the trouble is that no one wants to take a noisy and unruly parrot as well as myself!"

"No, I suppose not."

Lyndon noticed that the parrot was still looking at him menacingly.

"And I will not go without Pickle," she continued, "as he is all the family that is left to me in the world."

"Of course. I absolutely understand."

He did not, but he could tell by the determined look in her blue eyes and the way that she held her pointed chin high on her slender neck that she meant what she said.

And then the image of a little monkey in a red coat, being cosseted and caressed by an aristocratic old woman, came to him.

He had felt guilty about not visiting the Contessa at her hotel. Had she waited for him there? Perhaps she had forgotten all about him and found other English people to befriend her.

But this glorious girl might be able to help her and the old Contessa, who loved her monkey so much, might even understand this girl's attachment to her parrot.

He dug in his pocket and pulled out the Contessa's card.

"I don't know if this will be any use," he said. "but I believe this person may be seeking a companion."

"You are too kind, Mr. Jones!"

The girl's face lit up as she took the card from him.

"Not at all."

Lyndon could now hear heavy footsteps hurrying along the wharf behind him towards *The Grace Darling*.

For all the time he had been talking to this girl, he had forgotten all about Venice.

If he was not careful, he would miss the departure he had been so impatiently waiting for.

"I have to go," he blurted out. "It has been such a pleasure to meet you."

"Yes. Thank you, again."

The girl reached out her hand, but he was already on his way.

There was a strange feeling in Lyndon's heart as he climbed back on board *The Grace Darling*.

Something about this lovely girl touched his heart and he did not know if he could bear it.

He did not dare look back at the wharf in case she was still there, standing by the water with the last light of the evening gleaming on her golden hair.

# CHAPTER SEVEN

"*Let me out*! *Let me out*!" a small voice cried.

It was very early, but Pickle was already awake.

Last night Rosella had been feeling so tired that she had forgotten to pull the blanket over his cage and the rays of the rising sun had shone through the tiny window of the garret where they were staying and awakened him.

She rolled over on the lumpy mattress that lay on the floorboards and gave him a piece of bread from her last night's supper.

"*Can I have a nut*?" he asked, looking at the bread with his head on one side.

"Shh, now Pickle!" Rosella whispered. "We must not wake the baby!"

But it was too late. From downstairs she could hear that young Peter was already starting to cry.

Sarah, the sister-in-law of Thomas, the gardener's boy, had been delighted to take Rosella in.

Her husband, a sailor, was away on a long voyage and with two small children and a new baby, she was very glad of the money that Rosella could give her.

But the cottage where they lived was very crowded and Pickle was nervous of the children.

And he nipped their fingers when they tried to push their little hands through the bars of his cage to stroke him.

And so Rosella had to keep him in the garret, which was so small and cramped that she could only just stand up right in the very middle of the one room.

If she left him on his own, he would scream loudly and call for her, which was most unpleasant for Sarah and her family, so whenever Rosella went out from the cottage, he had to go with her.

She sighed as she thought about the many hours she had spent walking along the streets of London, carrying the heavy parrot cage, as she tried to find someone who would offer her employment.

Several agencies, which found positions for young ladies, had produced introductions for her, in spite of the fact that she had no experience of being a Governess or a lady's companion.

Rosella's charming manners and well-spoken voice meant that many of the potential employers she had visited would have been happy to take her on.

But Pickle, alas, did not have these assets and there was no one at all who would be prepared to offer the noisy bird a home alongside his Mistress.

"What shall we do?" Rosella asked him, as the bird reluctantly began to nibble on a piece of dry bread. "Sarah is very kind, but we cannot stay here for ever."

Downstairs Sarah's children had also woken up and were shouting for their breakfast.

Rosella got up from her mattress and washed her face and hands in the cracked bowl Sarah had given her.

Then she put on her favourite blue dress and began to comb her hair.

'I must not be despondent,' she now told herself. 'I must carry on, bravely and smiling.'

She thought with longing of the picture she had left behind hanging on her bedroom wall.

If only she could see that young man's happy smile this morning. Surely he would give her the strength and courage to set off again and find her way forward.

But she would never see him again, as she could never go back to New Hall.

Sadly Rosella picked up the old coat that Thomas had given her from where she had laid it on the floor last night, as there was no place to hang clothes in the garret.

She was just folding it and laying it on the mattress, when she recalled what had happened when she walked down to the river last night.

She had met a young man with a handsome face not so very different from the man in the painting, except that, in spite of the outlandish cloak and big hat – which would not have looked at all out of place in a painting – this was a very real person with black hair and brown eyes.

Because of his eyes and his strange clothes, Rosella had assumed that he was a foreigner and she smiled, as she remembered how surprised she was when he spoke to her in perfect English.

Then she recalled what he had given her.

Rosella fumbled in the pocket of the coat and found the small rectangle of cardboard – the calling card of a Contessa from Italy.

Rosella's heart sank a little at the thought of having to face yet another interview and another rejection.

It was kind of the young man to give her this, but surely a Contessa, who lived in a Palazzo, would have no time for a very young English girl, who had no experience and a very noisy parrot she would not be parted from.

When Rosella went down the stairs to help Sarah give the two small children their breakfast, the sailor's wife told her to be cheerful and not to give up.

"You go and see this Contessa, whoever she is," she said, spooning bread and milk into the mouth of young Kate. "Keep tryin', that's the only way. Not that I don't like to have you here in spite of that dreadful old bird. But you'll never get anythin' if you don't keep tryin'."

Rosella was watching over little Johnny, who was only just old enough to be responsible for his own bowl and spoon at mealtimes, but who sometimes forgot himself and threw the whole lot on the floor.

She looked around at the crowded kitchen, where Sarah spent most of every day, cooking and washing and looking after the young ones and then, when they had gone to sleep, working at the sewing she took in to make a little extra money.

There were no parlourmaids or housekeepers here. And no money unless you worked for it.

And all over the East End of London, there were thousands upon thousands of similar houses where families worked and struggled to make a living.

Rosella might have her little bag of gold sovereigns now, but it would not last for ever. She must do as Sarah advised and keep going to try to find some paid work.

Johnny was pushing his bowl towards the edge of the table, a broad smile on his little face and with his thick fringe of fair hair, he reminded her very much of Thomas, back at New Hall.

"Careful," she said, rescuing the bowl. "Have you finished, Johnny?"

"Yes!" he told her and he jumped down from the chair and began running round the kitchen, shouting, "you naughty, naughty boy!" in a good imitation of Pickle.

Rosella and his mother could not help laughing at him, until the noise of his shouting became unbearable and they let him out to play in the back yard.

"I'm sorry," Rosella said. "It's usually the other way round. Pickle hears things and copies them!"

"Your bird is just like a child," Sarah replied, "only one that never grows up. You will never be able to send him off to school and he will never leave home to earn his own living."

Little Katie had finished her bread and milk now, and her mother sat back and took a long drink from her cup of tea.

But Sarah's relaxation was interrupted by the loud wails of a crying baby from upstairs.

"What's that?" Sarah asked, looking very puzzled. "I can hear Peter crying, but he's lying over there as happy as can be?"

"I am afraid it's Pickle again!" Rosella laughed. "He's fed up with waiting for me and he's trying out a new imitation to see if will bring me running to him. I expect he has seen how we rush to pick up Peter when he cries."

"Well I never," sighed Sarah. "You should put that bird in a circus."

Rosella smiled to herself. Of course, if you wanted Pickle to say or do something on demand, he never would.

He would just sit silently and glare at the circus-goers and they would all demand their money back.

"I will get him out of your way," she said to Sarah, "and take him with me to see the Contessa."

"Good luck," Sarah said. "P'raps the old lady has a sense of humour. You might be lucky, this time."

*

Rosella did not feel as if luck was on her side, as she stood by the marble reception desk in the lobby of *The Palace Hotel* in Bayswater.

The clerk at the desk looked at her disapprovingly through his *pince-nez*.

"I cannot allow you to remain in this hotel, miss," he said. "You must remove yourself and that – creature – immediately!"

"*Good afternoon*!" Pickle squawked and several of the well-dressed ladies and gentlemen passing through the lobby laughed and pointed at the bird.

The clerk was not impressed and continued to glare at Rosella.

"I *must* see the Contessa Allegrini," she explained. "I have come a long way, especially to speak to her."

She thought of the very long journey across London from Limehouse on the omnibus, carrying Pickle's heavy cage on her knee and knew that she could not face going back to Sarah's cottage without at least having spoken to the Contessa.

"Is the lady expecting you?" the clerk asked with a sniff. "Do you have an appointment?"

"No," Rosella replied and held out the Contessa's card. "But an acquaintance of hers recommended I should call on her and he gave me this."

The clerk shook his head, looking crossly at Pickle, who was now muttering to himself and preening his wings.

"I am afraid I must ask you to leave. We cannot have this kind of thing at *The Palace Hotel*."

Several of the passers-by had stopped by Pickle's cage and were peering at him. A gentleman reached down to poke a finger through the bars and before Rosella could warn him, Pickle had bitten his finger.

The gentleman shook his hand and laughed good-humouredly, but the clerk was furious.

He came bustling round to the front of the desk and confronted Rosella.

"Out!" he hissed. "You are causing a disturbance and inconveniencing our guests. Out!"

He picked up Pickle's cage and made as if to fling it across the lobby and out of the front door of the hotel.

Rosella quickly pulled the parrot's cage out of his hands before he could do so. It was clearly no use trying to persuade him to let her see the Contessa.

She would just have to go back to Limehouse.

She was about to make her way out of the hotel, pursued by the infuriated clerk, when there was a jangling, rattling noise and a hubbub of women's voices from the other side of the lobby.

The hotel lift was descending to the ground floor packed with a full load of passengers.

The gilded gates crashed open and a small woman dressed in black, surrounded by three white-capped maids, emerged.

Rosella put down the birdcage and then watched in amazement as this woman, who was clearly very old and frail and carried a stick with a gold handle, marched up to the reception desk and began to ring the bell.

She was shouting loudly in a foreign language that Rosella could not understand and she seemed very angry indeed about something.

All the other guests in the lobby were staring at her with their mouths open, but no one made any attempt to speak to the woman.

The clerk scurried back to his post behind the desk, looking harassed.

"Contessa," he began, struggling to get a word in edgeways. "What is the matter now?"

"*Limone*! *Mi piace il te con limone, stupido*!" the woman shrilled at the top of her voice and then launched into another torrent of words, as her white-capped maids stood around looking helpless.

Rosella could not help but think that all of this was far more of a disturbance than she and Pickle had caused.

At last the clerk seemed to have understood what the woman was trying to say.

"I am so sorry, Contessa," he said, "we will send up some lemon for your tea at once. How regrettable that it should have been forgotten – again."

"*Vergogna*! You are a disgrace!" the woman said with an imperious nod of her grey head and she turned to go back to the lift, followed by her attendants.

'*Contessa*?' Rosella caught her breath. 'Surely this little woman must be the Contessa Allegrini.'

But it was too late to speak to her as they were all inside the lift and the porter was pulling the gates closed.

Just before the gilded gates had rattled shut, a small creature shot out of the lift and bounded across the lobby towards Rosella.

The Contessa gave a loud shriek.

"*Aiuta*! *Auita*!"

Pickle gave a loud squeal and flapped his wings.

"*Goodness me*!" he cawed, his round eyes bulging with alarm.

A small monkey, dressed in a red silk coat, had run up to the cage and was now peering through the bars and chattering at Pickle.

Much to Rosella's surprise, Pickle did not scream or try to bite the monkey. Instead, he nodded his head as if in greeting and then squawked,

*"Hello!"*

The monkey jumped up and down in excitement as Pickle ran along his perch, saying *"can I have a nut?"* – his favourite phrase, which he had uttered in vain many times over the last few days, for there were no nuts to be had at Sarah's cottage.

Rosella watched in amazement as the little monkey reached into a pocket at the side of its coat and produced a peanut, which it passed through the bars of the cage.

Pickle seized the peanut with his beak and then held it in his foot, as he did with all his treats, while he nibbled on it with great enjoyment.

The monkey crouched down and watched him with its mournful brown eyes.

Something tapped Rosella on the shoulder and she jumped in alarm.

It was the old woman's walking stick.

"Who are you?" she then demanded in a harsh thick accent, her black eyes blazing fiercely. "And what are you doing with my Pepe?"

"Nothing, ma'am," Rosella began, but before she could explain what had happened, the old woman poked at her with her stick, pushing her away from the monkey.

"Oh – you little vagabond! You would steal him – is that it?"

"No, no, not at all – I was just – "

"Oh yes, you may have the face of an angel, but I know your kind!"

She smacked Rosella's legs with her stick, trying to drive her out of the lobby.

One of the Contessa's maids caught Pepe and was holding him tightly in her arms.

Rosella was almost out of the hotel door and on the street when cries of a very unhappy baby filled the lobby.

Everyone looked around in surprise and the maids bustled about, searching for the unfortunate child.

Even the Contessa stopped hounding Rosella and turned around to see what was going on.

"*Waaaa – aaaah*!" Pickle cried, standing on tiptoe on his perch and straining to see where Rosella had gone.

"It's all right!" she called to him. "I won't leave you!"

"*Oh, meravigliosa*!" One of the maids had spotted the birdcage. "*Un papagallo*!"

She pointed at Pickle, one hand held to her mouth in amazement.

The clerk came from behind his desk again.

"This is not a menagerie!" he shouted out, running towards Rosella. "I have asked you to leave several times, miss! Now *go*!"

The Contessa held out her stick to block his path.

"*Momento*!" she said to him and then she looked at Rosella. "It's your bird, yes, that makes this crying?"

Rosella nodded.

"Incredible," the old woman shook her head. "Tell me – how you teach him this?"

"Oh – I don't," Rosella replied. "He just does it, he copies whatever he hears."

"And what else does he say?" the Contessa asked.

"All kinds of things, but – "

Rosella was about to explain that Pickle sometimes went very quiet if strangers stared at him and expected him to speak to them, when he interrupted her.

"*Is it time for tea?*" he asked in Aunt Beatrice's voice.

The Countess stared at him with her bright black eyes and then she threw back her head and laughed.

"*Si, si! Ha ragione, Signore Papagallo!* It is indeed time for tea."

She rapped her stick on the marble floor and called to the clerk.

"Please bring *Signore Papagallo* to my room," she ordered him. "He is my honoured guest. And you, girl, I suppose you had better come too."

Her heart beating fast, Rosella followed the clerk as he carried Pickle up the wide staircase to the Contessa's luxurious suite.

Rosella almost wept when she saw the tea that had been laid out for the Contessa and her attendants.

There were cucumber sandwiches and little cakes iced with pink and violet sugar, there were thick slices of rich fruitcake and a Victoria sponge as light as those that Mrs. Dawkins used to make.

She hardly dared to taste any of it, as the memories that came flooding back to her of happy teatimes at New Hall, were very painful.

Pickle, on the other hand, accepted many crumbs of cake and a whole ginger biscuit from the Contessa's own hand.

But he seemed to prefer peanuts and almonds, for as soon as the monkey's tiny fingers held one of these out to him, Pickle let all the other delicacies fall to the bottom of his cage.

He so entranced the Contessa that she completely ignored Rosella until tea was almost over.

But she was happy to just sit and look around at all the beautiful objects that filled the elegant hotel room.

There were exquisite lace clothes laid out over the tables that matched the delicate edging of the maid's caps and aprons.

The tall glass vases, which held great bouquets of roses and lilies, were made of swirls and twists of bright colours, red and purple and gold.

Rosella had never seen anything like them before.

And everywhere, from the dangling gems that hung from the Contessa's ears to the great embroidered cloth that was draped over the sofa, there was gold.

"You don't like your food, miss?" the Contessa's harsh voice spoke next to Rosella.

"Oh – it's quite lovely, thank you, but I have little appetite," Rosella replied.

The old woman frowned at her.

"Who are you?" she asked. "What is your name?"

"My name is – Jane," Rosella replied.

The Contessa shook her head.

"*Ja-ane*! I don't like your English names, but you seem like a well-bred girl. So why are you dressed like a *poverina*, a poor little one with nothing and nobody?"

Rosella looked down at her dark cotton dress.

It was certainly looking distinctly shabby from the long journey from Hampshire and from all the time she had spent caring for Sarah's children and tramping around the City looking for work.

"I came to find you, ma'am," she said and pulled out the card the young man had given her. "I am looking for work and a – friend told me that you might be able to help me."

The Contessa took the card and spoke at length in Italian as she saw the writing on it and then she turned to Rosella,

"Where did you get this?" she demanded.

Rosella explained about the charming young man she had spoken to on the banks of the Thames and, as she described his face and his strange clothes, she remembered how he had looked at her with his dark eyes and she had felt her cheeks grow a little warm.

The Contessa shook her head.

"Ah, that wicked boy! I waited – and he did not come. So you know him? He is a friend of yours?"

"No, but he kindly gave me your card. And – "

Rosella felt anxiety rise in chest as she continued,

" – he said that you might need a companion, while you are in London, ma'am"

"No!" The Contessa tossed her head. "Soon I will be going back to my home in Italy and so I have no need of anyone. But – "

She pointed at the birdcage.

The monkey had reached its arm through the bars and was scratching the top of Pickle's head, as the parrot blinked his eyes in absolute bliss.

"I will have your *papagallo*," she said. "My Pepe loves him. Perhaps the bird will keep him from straying. How much do you want for him."

"No!" Rosella cried and her heart turned over with fear. "I could not part with Pickle!"

The Contessa's eyes flashed and then she gestured to one of the maids to bring her a gilded wooden box.

"Don't you know I am one of the richest women in Italy?" the Contessa snapped. "Whatever your price, I will pay it."

Rosella thought for a moment. Never in her wildest dreams had she considered leaving England, but what was there now to stay for?

She took a deep breath and looked straight into the Contessa's deep-set eyes.

"If he goes with you, then I must go too! That is my price, ma'am."

The Contessa raised her eyebrows.

"You don't want my gold?" she said and ran her fingers through the coins that filled the box. "You strange girl."

"I cannot be parted from Pickle," Rosella said once more. "He is – all I have."

The Contessa stared at her for a long moment and then she said,

"Very well. I agree your price. You and your bird will come to my home. We leave day after tomorrow."

*

Lyndon sighed with relief as the rowing boat pulled out of the Port of Mestre to take him on the last stage of his journey.

Every inch of him felt gritty with coal dust, even though he had not had to handle any of the sacks, which even now were being unloaded from *The Grace Darling* into carts that lined the side of the dock.

He rubbed his tired eyes and thought longingly of the room he would soon be occupying and the bath that he would soon be able to have in one of the boarding houses in a not-too-expensive district of Venice.

He might find a place in *Canareggio* perhaps or even in *Guidecca*. He whispered the names to himself, practising the pronunciation of the unfamiliar sounds.

The boat was fairly flying through the water as the two boatmen who plied the oars were strong solid men.

Lyndon looked up and then caught his breath in amazement.

He had imagined his first sight of Venice so many times, but nothing he had pictured could equal the vision that now opened up before him.

It was evening and the sun was hanging low in the sky like a huge orb of fire, turning the whole expanse of the sky to glittering gold.

All around him the waters of the Lagoon rippled, stretching away like a sheet of beaten silver.

Straight ahead on the horizon, silhouetted against the glowing sky, were the domes and towers and fretted rooftops of a distant City.

A City that looked just as if it belonged in another world – a more outlandish and extravagant and beautiful world than the one that Lyndon knew.

At last he had come to Venice.

'This is where my life begins,' he whispered and he clutched the side of the boat and strained to see more as the sun sank down in the sky.

# CHAPTER EIGHT

"*Dear Thomas, I am writing to let you know that all is well with me – "*

Rosella dipped the gold nib of her pen into the blue glass inkbottle that stood on the writing desk.

She wanted to tell Thomas about the extraordinary place where she had now been living for a whole week, but how could she possibly describe the Ca' degli Angeli – the great sumptuous Palazzo, home to the Contessa Allegrini, without using too many long words?

She was sitting by the window of her bedroom, one of the smaller rooms in the old building, yet it was almost twice the size of her room at New Hall.

Below her, through the open shutters, she could see the deep green water of the Grand Canal and the sunlight flashing on the waves that rippled every time a boat drifted past.

"*I am in Venice*," she wrote, "*and I have just seen a gondola*," but then she realised that Thomas would have no idea what she meant.

"*There is nothing like it in England*, she continued. "*It is a sort of long boat with a carved prow and a high stern and the ladies and gentlemen of Venice lie back on velvet cushions while the gondolier stands at the back and steers and rows with just one long oar*!

*There are no roads here in Venice, everything and everyone must travel by water on the canals.*"

She was then about to describe the fabulous, gold-painted furniture that filled her bedroom at the Palazzo and the delicious food that was laid out every day on the great table in the dining room – and, most of all, she wanted to tell Thomas about the Contessa.

But she put down the pen to think.

What if someone found the letter and, even though she signed it just with the words '*your friend*', realised who had sent it?

She could not take the risk of someone from New Hall tracing her to Venice and to the Ca' degli Angeli.

"*I cannot say more, Thomas, except that I am very happy and I am staying in a beautiful Palazzo – which is Italian, of course, for Palace – with someone who is very kind to me,*" she continued.

"*I hope that all is well with you.  I think of you often and send you my good wishes.  My kindest thoughts too go to your sister, I am so grateful to her for her help.*

*Your friend.*"

With a pang in her heart that she could not write her own name below her words of gratitude, she then folded the thick velvety paper.

She sealed the letter with a blob of red sealing wax and rang the bell for Mimi, the young maid the Contessa had assigned to her and, as she waited for the girl to knock at the tall oak door of her bedroom, she thought how sad it was that the only one she could tell about her adventures was the gardener's boy.

Sarah would be pleased to know that all was well with Rosella, but she could not read, so there was no point in sending a letter to her until her husband came home.

If only Rosella knew where that young man, Mr. Jones, lived, the mysterious black-cloaked person who had given her the Contessa's card.

She would have liked so much to tell him that she

was here in Venice and to thank him for the introduction.

Rosella felt her face grow warm as it always did when she thought about him. She could not forget the way that his dark eyes had looked into hers and the way that his voice had made her feel.

But she did not even know his name.

"*Signorina*?"

Mimi was by her side, her round face glowing like a warm peach.

Rosella scribbled Thomas's name on the letter and addressed it to *New Hall, Near Winchester, England, care of the Head Gardener*, as she was sure that he would not recognise her writing.

She gave the letter to Mimi.

"*Tua famiglia in Inghilterra*?" Mimi then asked, looking curiously at the address.

"No, not my family," Rosella replied, for already she was beginning to understand just a little of the Italian language. "Just a friend. *Un amico*."

"A-ah!" Mimi smiled at her. "*Un amico*."

And she hurried off to post the letter, pressing it to her heart.

Rosella thought about her letter wending its way to England and then tears sprang into her eyes as she pictured Thomas opening it in the Rose Garden, hiding from prying eyes under the masses of scented blooms.

There was a rap at her door.

"Ja-ane!" an imperious voice called out. "Is your window closed?"

Rosella jumped up and pulled the heavy window shut, just in time, for the Contessa did not hesitate before entering the room with Pepe sitting on one shoulder and

Pickle on the other, nibbling affectionately at her earring.

"*Hello, my dear!*" the parrot shouted, when he saw Rosella and then he flew right up and perched on top of the embroidered curtain that surrounded her four-poster bed.

"Come down, you naughty Pickle," she told him, hastily wiping her eyes, so that the Contessa should not see that she had been crying.

"Oh, he is so happy to be flying free," the Contessa said. "Leave him, but what is the matter? You are upset?"

"It's nothing really," Rosella sniffed.

She was still a little apprehensive of the Contessa, for the old woman could fall into a tempestuous rage at the least excuse.

And Rosella could not quite forget the way that the Contessa had attacked her with her walking stick in the lobby of *The Palace Hotel* and also, how she had not really wanted Rosella to come to Italy with her – since she was only interested in Pickle the talking parrot.

All through the voyage to Venice on the beautiful ship *La Maschera*, Rosella had made herself very useful, arranging the flowers in the Contessa's luxurious cabin and keeping watch over Pepe.

And when they arrived, it seemed that she had gone up in the Contessa's esteem, as she had been allocated this beautiful room, overlooking the Grand Canal and she was always invited to dine with the old woman.

Now the Contessa was staring at her intently.

"Jane," she began. "Something is troubling you, I can see. *Un segreto*? A secret you speak of to no one?"

Rosella's limbs grew cold with fear.

"Please," she replied, "Really, there is nothing that troubles me. I am so happy to be here and you are so very kind to me, ma'am."

"But who are you?" the Contessa frowned. "I think you are not what you seem."

"I am Jane – " Rosella began, but Pickle interrupted her by flying down and landing on her head.

"Ouch! Do be careful," she scolded him, lifting her hand for him to step down.

He promptly flew off again and landed on the table. Pepe then jumped down from the Contessa's shoulder and bounded over to join him.

Pickle bowed his head and Pepe sat down next to him and began combing the feathers on the back of the bird's neck with his tiny fingers.

The Contessa laughed.

"Oh, your bird! So clever. But Jane, can you tell me why, when you left the room this morning, he said, '*Bye bye, Rosella*'."

Rosella's cheeks burned at her words.

She had not heard Pickle say this today, but then she remembered that he had done so sometimes in the past, when Aunt Beatrice was still alive.

Without meaning to, the parrot had betrayed her.

The Contessa had seen her blush.

"I thought so! *You* are this mysterious Rosella, are you not! I give thanks, for never again will I have to make that horrible English sound – *Ja-ane*."

"No, please, you must not call me Rosella."

"Why are you so afraid?"

"I don't want anyone to know I am here."

"But your family?"

"I have no family. There was only my aunt and she

died."

"Oh, *povera!*" the Contessa reached out and patted Rosella's hair. "But why did she not leave you her fortune, this aunt? Why did she leave you to go out in the world at mercy of strangers?"

Rosella then explained that Aunt Beatrice had died suddenly and the estate had gone to her husband's brother.

"I have nothing now," she whispered.

The Contessa's black eyes glowed.

"No one who has a good friend has nothing," she exclaimed and then she sighed,

"You poor creature. You have face of angel and the kindness of one too. You are patient with my naughty Pepe. And you love beautiful things – I have watched how tenderly you touch flowers when you put them into vases for me."

Tears sprang into Rosella's eyes, as she thought of the daily ritual she used to perform at New Hall.

"I-I used to arrange the flowers for my aunt," she explained.

"Of course," the Contessa responded, her own eyes suddenly bright, "but you must not feel sad. A pretty girl like you – you must have handsome young man – a suitor – who waits for you in England?"

Rosella shook her head.

She could not bring herself to speak of the horrible Mr. Merriman, who was neither young nor handsome.

A determined look came over the Contessa's face.

"The time of *Carnivale* is past now for this year, but I am going to hold a ball. *Un Ballo in Maschera*! And I shall ask all the Nobility of Venice and English visitors to come. And we shall see if we cannot find you a handsome suitor – Rosella!"

"Oh, surely you don't mean that, I-I couldn't."

Rosella recoiled in horror at the thought of having to attend a ball.

The Contessa laughed.

"Of course you can," she persisted. "No one will recognise you, as you will be masked. But none the less, you cannot fail to catch the eye of the young men."

She clapped her hands imperiously.

"Come, there will be no argument."

The Contessa called out at the top of her voice for Giovanni, the gondolier who ferried her about the City.

"Go to Signora Taglioni at once," she told him, when he came to the door.

She snatched a piece of paper from the desk and scribbled something onto it.

"Give her this – and tell her the appointment must be as soon as possible. Tomorrow!"

*

Next morning, Rosella stood outside one of the side doors of the Palazzo, looking down into the dark water of a narrow waterway that branched off from the Grand Canal.

"*Signorina?*"

Giovanni, a tall, well-built man with thick black hair and a wide smile, held out his strong hand to help her down into the gondola.

He was the brother of Mimi, her maid, and she was sure that he was a good trustworthy man, but still Rosella felt a little uneasy.

"Where are we going?" she asked him.

He laughed and shook his head,

"*Segreto.*"

A little rush of panic surged in Rosella's chest.

She had never been in a gondola before and here she was about to step into one all on her own to be carried away to an unknown destination.

She did not want to go and she turned to run back inside the Palazzo, but then her heart leapt with shock, for there right next to her at the side of the door was a life-size statue of a young man.

The white stone was worn and dirty, but she could see that his carved face was handsome and he wore a large turban on his head.

Rosella gasped.

"Who is that?" she asked.

Giovanni shrugged.

"*Non lo so.* I don't know. *Antico, antico.* From a long time ago. Come, Signorina. We must not be late for your appointment."

The statue's curved lips seem to smile at Rosella.

"*Go*," they seemed to say. "*Go on – and see what awaits you.*"

Her heart in her mouth, she allowed Giovanni to help her into the swaying gondola and then she lay back on the cushions, as he expertly steered the slender craft over the dark water and out onto the Grand Canal.

*

Lyndon knelt up in the prow of the rowing boat, gazing at the domes and roofs of Venice, gleaming under the morning sun.

He knew that he should sit down to steady the boat, but he was so excited by what he had just found in the Cemetery of San Michele, that he simply could not contain himself.

And the placid oarsman, pulling steadily at the oars, did not seem to mind that his passenger was acting like an over-excited child.

Since he had come to Venice, Lyndon had looked across the water many times to the mysterious island of San Michele, where the dark spires of the cypress trees towered over the cemetery walls.

Since he had arrived in Venice, Lyndon had wasted no time in seeing all the sights. He had marvelled at the glories of St. Mark's Square with its Basilica and its tall Campanile.

He had wandered alone through the dark alleyways, crossing tiny bridges over the canals and found glory upon glory of art and architecture to astonish him.

But the most extraordinary experience of all had been today at the cemetery of Venice.

As he strolled among all the tombs and monuments, admiring the carved angels and the exquisite inscriptions commemorating the famous families of Venice, he thought he might hunt among some of the smaller gravestones and see if he could find some English names.

And there he had found, clearly carved on a marble headstone, the words,

*"In memory of Lord Osborne Brockley, 1786."*

Lyndon's heart was in his mouth as he read this, for Lord Osborne had been brother to his great-grandfather.

He had never taken much interest in the history of his family, but he did recall some story of Lord Osborne leaving England to embark on a Grand Tour of Europe – and never returning.

The rumour was that he had had an unhappy love affair and had then drowned.

Lyndon knelt down and laid his hand on the warm marble. Perhaps his great-uncle had lost his life here in the silvery waters of the Lagoon.

'Rest in peace,' he whispered to Lord Osborne's grave and then closed his eyes for a moment in the warm sunshine.

As he stepped back into the rowing boat and began the short journey back to the City, his heart pounded with excitement.

What an extraordinary coincidence it was, that he should be following in the footsteps of his ancestor!

But there was no way that he, Lyndon, would fall victim to an unhappy love affair.

He had done his sightseeing now. San Michele was the last place on the list.

Now he should mingle a little in Society and meet some of the beautiful women of Venice – not to fall in love with, oh no! – but to flirt with and enjoy some liaisons that would not in any way touch his heart.

A rowing boat had come out from the mouth of one of the canals and was coming towards him.

Lyndon looked over and almost laughed out loud, as it was as if his wish to meet a lovely woman had just become a reality.

Sitting in the front of the rowing boat was a slender young girl. She was not dark like all the Italian girls, but gloriously fair with a cloud of gold hair around her head that shone under the morning sun like a bright halo.

Where was the boat taking her, all on her own on this beautiful morning?

As they drew closer, he saw that she was looking at him and she was even lovelier that he had first thought, for her skin was pale and her face exquisitely shaped.

She was staring at him so intently that, as they drew closer, he decided to stand up and call a greeting across to her.

She really was very lovely indeed.

And then his heart stopped still with shock, as he had seen her somewhere before.

But where? He could not quite remember, although he was sure it was not here, in Venice, that they had met.

\*

"Don't be afraid, *Signorina*," Giovanni said in his thick Italian accent.

They had come to the edge of the tall buildings and were looking out over a wide expanse of shining water.

At the edge of the water a small blue rowing boat was tied and Giovanni now walked towards it, beckoning for her to follow him.

"Come, come!" he urged.

Reluctantly Rosella followed, asking, for the tenth time, where he was taking her, but he would only smile and nod mysteriously.

Now she was in the rowing boat and it was pushing through the water. Ahead lay a walled island with tall trees growing straight upwards.

It looked like a great house or Palace of some kind, but when Rosella asked Giovanni who lived there, he just frowned and shook his head as he pulled on the oars.

Another small rowing boat, coming the other way, had just left the island and Rosella could now see that a tall figure in a wide hat and long cloak was on board.

She could not see the face of this person, as the sun was in her eyes, but surely – it had to be – the same young man she had met by the banks of the River Thames!

As the boats drew level, he stood up and grinned at her, his dark eyes flashing, a bold expression on his face.

It *was* him!

And yet – he seemed so very different – not at all the same charming man she remembered from Limehouse.

"Hey!" he called out. *"Buon giorno, bellissima!"*

Giovanni gave a disapproving grunt and tugged at the oars, so that their boat shot past, leaving the young man behind.

He must have forgotten that he had met her before in England and Rosella's heart felt touched with ice.

She had mused about him every day, but clearly he had not been thinking of her.

She must put his face, which had stayed so vividly in her thoughts, right out of her mind.

There was no use at all in thinking of him anymore.

Ahead of the walled island there was another bigger island and that was where they were heading.

Soon Giovanni was tying up the boat and offering his arm to Rosella to help her ashore.

"Murano," he said proudly, gesturing at the quiet streets and squares that stretched ahead in the sunshine.

Rosella followed him along the quayside, passing shop windows filled with displays of the same beautiful striped and swirled glass the Contessa's vases and wine glasses were made from.

And in one building where the door stood open to reveal the dark interior, she saw a man blowing into a long tube and on the end of the tube a great blob of glass was forming, as if he was blowing a bubble.

Giovanni would not let her linger. He urged her on until they reached a large house on one of the squares.

Outside two old women sat on wooden chairs, their nimble fingers flicking over cushions on which they were creating intricate patterns of delicate lace.

Giovanni knocked on the door and, as it opened, she saw that inside there was rack upon rack of silks in every colour of the rainbow.

She had come to a dressmaker's shop!

A tall woman in a black gown with straight dark hair pulled back into bun approached.

"Rosella!" she began in a deep voice. *"La Rosa d'Inghilterra* – the English Rose! I am Signora Taglioni, the Contessa's dressmaker, we have been waiting for you."

She selected a bolt of silk and Rosella shivered, for it was exactly the same colour as the dress in her vision.

For a moment she thought she might faint again. But Signora Taglioni smiled kindly at her as the sun shone through the windows onto the rose-pink silk.

There was nothing to be afraid of, Rosella thought.

Maybe her vision had been just a little glimpse into the future and it was only herself that she had seen in that shadowy ballroom –

She stepped forward to allow Signora Taglioni to drape the silk around her.

\*

A few days later, Lyndon sat in one of the *cafés* in St. Mark's Square, sipping a cup of the strong bitter Italian coffee he had grown to love so much.

He kept his hat pulled down over his eyes, for this was a place much frequented by travellers, many of them English.

He had thought often of the lovely girl he had seen on his way back from San Michele – and had come to the conclusion that, with her fair colouring, she was probably an English girl.

Maybe she was visiting Venice with her family and had been on her way to the world famous glass factories of Murano to buy gifts and trinkets to take home.

If he sat here long enough, she was bound to walk by and, if he was lucky, she might be with her brothers and sisters and not with her Mama and Papa and he might have a chance to speak to her.

Lyndon shook himself.

He really was being very silly. There were so many other girls. So why could he not stop thinking about this particular one?

For example there was now a most comely girl with pink cheeks and shining brown hair sitting at the table next to him.

With her was an older woman in a large velvet hat with a bunch of wax cherries pinned to the side.

"Oh, can we not go, Mama?" the girl was saying in a beguiling voice. "A masked ball sounds so exciting."

Lyndon remembered how he had dreamed of going to a masked ball back in London long before he had come to Venice, as he listened to the older woman's response.

She was shaking her head now, so that the cherries bobbed up and down.

"I don't think so, my darling."

The girl pouted.

"But Mama – it's so kind of the Contessa Allegrini to invite us. She is one of the most important people in Venice."

"A masked ball is not a suitable event, Isabel, for a young girl like yourself to attend. And that is the end of it."

She looked at Lyndon in his disreputable cloak and hat and realised that he was listening to their conversation. She then stood up and gave him a disapproving look from under the wobbling cherries.

"Now – where is that waiter? I think it is time we returned to our hotel, Isabel!" she asserted.

Lyndon's heart was pounding with excitement as he watched the two of them leave the *café*.

Contessa Allegrini! The old woman from the yacht *La Maschera*, whose monkey he had rescued.

And now at last he remembered where he had met the lovely girl with the angelic fair hair.

She had been standing by the river Thames with her parrot in its cage and he had given her the Contessa's card.

In the excitement of being in Venice and exploring the City, he had forgotten all about her.

Now he must waste no time in finding himself a suitable outfit and, of course, a mask.

And then there was the rather small matter of an invitation. But Lyndon had made many contacts now in the City and he had no doubt that one of them would be able to help him gain entry to the exclusive ball.

# CHAPTER NINE

"*Bellissima*!" the Contessa cried, as Rosella spun around, the ruffles of her pink silk skirts swirling across the stone tiles of the entrance hall.

All day long the Ca' degli Angeli had seen comings and goings – of workmen with ladders come to nail up the garlands of roses that the Contessa had decreed must hang from the high ceiling of the ballroom and caterers – stout women bearing trays of pastries and cakes.

The first arrival at the Palazzo, early that morning, had been Signora Taglioni bearing Rosella's gown.

It was nearly two weeks since the visit to Murano for her fitting and Rosella's hand shook as she unfolded the tissue paper and lifted the gown to look at it.

"It's so heavy!" she had cried, as the many folds of pale-pink silk, trimmed with extra fine silver cobwebs of Venetian lace, tumbled out of the wrappings.

"Now you are not a girl anymore," the Contessa laughed. "You are a woman, a *bella donna* and you must bear the weight if you wear a gown that befits a woman."

Later, as the hot afternoon drew to a close and the shadows began to lengthen, Rosella made herself ready for the ball.

She had to ask Mimi to lace her corset very tightly, as the waist of the gown was tiny and she had to walk up and down her bedroom to get used to the way the glorious cascades of silk and lace swung around her legs.

And now the Contessa had sent for her to come

down to the hall and show her the gown.

"Hold up your head! Walk slowly! *Lente, lente!*" she ordered, watching Rosella parade up and down until she was satisfied that her protégée had mastered the art of wearing the gown to perfection.

"*Bene*," she exclaimed at last. "Good, you have the walk. Now all you must do is learn to dance like a woman. But I shall leave that lesson to the gentlemen who will be queuing up for the honour of partnering you. Now wait. There is one more thing."

The Contessa then left the hall and Rosella's heart fluttered as the vast front door of the Palazzo creaked open and a troupe of men in blue coats, carrying violin and flute cases, were ushered in.

The musicians had arrived. It would not be long now before the ball would begin.

"Here! The finishing touch."

The Contessa now returned, holding in her hand an object made of black velvet and winking with diamonds and rubies.

"*La maschera!*"

Rosella put the mask on, so that the upper half of her face was covered.

At the same time she could still see quite clearly though the eye slits, but somehow the Palazzo looked a little different, rather more shadowy and mysterious.

Now the Contessa was beckoning her to follow.

It was time to go to the ballroom, the great mirrored chamber with painted walls, tall mirrors and chandeliers made of Murano glass.

Rosella had seen it in the daytime, but never before at night when all the candles were lit.

As she walked through the high double doors, she

felt as if she was stepping straight into a dream – into that vision she had seen so many weeks before in Winchester.

There were the deep shadows clinging to the walls and the soft glow of the vast chandeliers and there, flitting about at the edge of her vision, were the ghostly figures of the servants preparing for the guests who would soon be here.

Everything seemed very familiar, although she had only seen it in a dream.

\*

Lyndon chuckled to himself as the gondola drifted through the twilight. In what other City in the world could one roam about in such an outlandish costume as he was wearing this evening and attract almost no attention?

His friend, Fabio, who owned several coffee shops in the vicinity and who had found Lyndon his lodgings in the Canareggio district, had loaned him a Turkish outfit in pale blue silk with baggy trousers and a turban made from a long ribbon of cloth.

"I shall look ridiculous," he had argued, as Fabio wound the cloth around his head.

"On the contrary, *Signore Jones*," Fabio grinned. "It's a proud tradition for the milords – the gentlemen of England – to come to Venice and to wear disguise for *Il Ballo in Maschera*."

"But – Fabio – how will the beautiful girls take me seriously in this turban?"

"Ah, *Signore*. They will adore you, as you make a very handsome and most – how do you say it? – *dashing* Turk. They will be totally intrigued and delighted by your mysterious presence."

Lyndon had glanced at himself in the mirror and seen that it was true, he did not look as silly as he felt, but actually made quite a reasonably convincing impression of an Oriental with his tall lean figure and dark eyes.

Fabio grinned at him.

"And they say the Contessa is giving this ball for a very particular young Signorina, a mysterious girl who has been living at the Palazzo and is very beautiful, they say. Perhaps you will even get to dance with her."

Now lying back on the comfortable velvet cushions of the gondola, Lyndon knew, deep in his heart, that this mysterious creature must be the golden-haired girl from the Thames.

Of course she would dance with him!

He pulled his mask out of the pocket of the baggy trousers. It was time to put it on.

When he had done so, he lent over the edge of the slender craft to see if he could catch a glimpse of his reflection in the smooth water.

It took him a moment to realise that the pale figure that caught his eye in the dark water, its head wreathed in the dusky turban and its eyes hidden behind black velvet, was indeed himself.

Uneasy, he tried to see the figure more clearly, but the gondolier plied his oar, pushing the craft forward and the image broke and dispersed in the waves.

Lyndon looked up at the darkening sky. Surely the ball must have begun by now.

Fabio had suggested that he enter the Palazzo with a group of other guests, if possible, so that the servants at the door would not look too closely at his invitation, which was intended for a *Dottore di Monte*, an elderly man who no longer had the wish to attend balls and parties and who was happy to allow Fabio's friend to take his place.

The top floors of the Ca' degli Angeli were ablaze with lights as the gondola drew near and Lyndon's heart beat fast as he heard the faint sounds of laughter and music floating down to him on the warm evening air.

He had no trouble entering the Palazzo, for a noisy and somewhat overweight English gentleman, dressed in the diamond-patterned costume of Harlequin and wearing a comic white mask with a long nose, had just disembarked, almost overturning the gondola he arrived in.

Lyndon flinched instinctively as he heard the man's voice, remonstrating with the gondolier and calling him 'a clumsy oaf,' when it was he who had very nearly sunk the gondola.

But the disturbance meant that Lyndon was able to pass though the great wooden doors into the Palazzo with no more than a quick glance from the footmen on duty.

He was inside at last and about to join the throng of guests at his first *Ballo in Maschera*.

\*

Rosella's whole body was fizzing with excitement, as if the tiny bubbles that flew upwards through the glasses of champagne she had just drunk were racing through her veins.

She had danced with at least ten masked gentlemen and she had not the faintest idea who they were.

She could not even make out if they were English or Italian, as none had spoken to her, although they smiled and their eyes flashed through the slits in their masks.

She was just thinking that she should sit out the next waltz and rest, when someone caught her eye in the shadows at the side of the ballroom.

A man dressed in a striking pale-blue costume was watching her, his dark gaze glinting through a black mask that sat just beneath the edge of his silken turban.

It was the young man from the portrait.

Rosella clutched her throat, as her heart was beating so fast that she thought it might choke her.

He smiled and his teeth flashed white as he walked towards her, holding out his hand.

"You are utterly beautiful!" he began. "Please will you dance with me?"

She stood, frozen to the spot, for now the vision she had had of the vast ballroom, the dream of the woman in the pink dress, standing beneath a chandelier, was coming true.

Her skin turned cold with shock and then, as he stood rigid in front of her, still smiling, she was suddenly burning hot and she felt trapped and imprisoned behind the tight velvet mask that hid her face.

She put up her hand to pull it away from her face and he reached out and caught her wrist.

"Please, don't! Not yet. Dance with me – "

"I – can't – I – "

"What is it?" he frowned at her and then released her arm and gently touched her hair where it fell over her shoulder. "Is it because we have met before? I think we have, as I would know these angel's tresses anywhere."

"Please, stop – !"

"This is a *Ballo in Maschera*. All are strangers. None are known to each other. Forget that we may have spoken once. You must dance with me!"

He took her hand in one of his and with the other he clasped her slender silken waist.

And then they were flying across the wide floor of the ballroom, spinning and twisting like the wild strands of bright glass in the beautiful Venetian vases all round them.

For something inside Rosella felt as fragile and icy as glass. She felt unreal, dreamlike, as if she had become someone else and left her old shy self completely behind.

Her body felt so weak that if they had stopped, she would have fallen to the ground, unable to stand. Yet the young man's eyes, glowing at her through the slits in his mask, drew her after him like a magnet, whirling over the dance floor.

It was as if they were one being, as she knew before he spun her to the left or right what he was going to do.

Even before he had taken the next step, she knew whether he would move swiftly or slow down a little.

The music of the flutes and the violins seemed to pulse inside her soul, exactly as she had heard it so many weeks before in the dressmaker's shop in Winchester.

"You dance like an angel," he whispered, his voice sending a sweet thrill that ran through her body from her toes to her fingertips.

The music began to slow, to die down and the fire and excitement ebbed from her body, leaving her shivering and afraid.

"What is it, *bellisima*?"

He held her hand in his and guided her to the far end of the room, where tall windows overlooked the Grand Canal.

"Is something wrong?"

"I – don't know what is happening to me," she said.

He laughed.

"You have just been dancing with someone who thinks you are the prettiest girl in the room. That is nothing to be upset about, surely. Why are you shivering so? It's very warm tonight."

"I must – speak to you," she stammered.

"Speak away!"

His eyes shone through his mask.

The musicians were striking up another tune and people were crowding onto the floor once again.

Rosella flinched as one couple almost barged into them as the next dance began.

The young man pushed at the window where they stood and it opened a little, revealing a narrow balcony.

"We could slip out here for a moment, if you would like that."

They stepped out into the night and the damp breath of the canal rose up to meet them, filling Rosella's head with its cool freshness.

She pulled the clinging mask away from her face.

"Do you remember me?" she asked him.

He was silent for a moment, staring at her.

"Of course I do. Of course. Why do you look at me like that?"

Rosella shook her head.

How could she find the words to explain about her vision and the painting –

"You are – so beautiful," his deep voice cracked a little as he spoke. "It – unnerves me."

He swallowed and then continued,

"I came here because of you. I saw you in the boat by San Michele and at first I could not remember where I had seen you before. Then I heard the Contessa's name and someone told me she was giving a ball for a beautiful young girl – an English girl – her protégée.

"And then I knew you were the girl from the River Thames that day. The girl I had given the Contessa's card to. And I understood that you must be the girl everyone was talking about."

He lifted her fingers and kissed them gently and, as she felt the tender warmth of his lips against her silk glove, a sensation as clear and bright as a flickering candle flame ran over her skin.

"Something is still wrong, what is it?" he said after a moment.

"I have to tell you – " she faltered. "Yes, we have met before, but – there is more to it than that – "

She gripped his hand in hers, suddenly fearful that, when he heard what she had to say, he might run away and leave her alone on the balcony above the Grand Canal.

Trembling, forcing herself to speak the words, she told him of the portrait that hung on her bedroom wall of the young man who looked so much like he did.

She explained about her aunt dying and her lack of fortune and her uncle's insistence that she marry a man she utterly disliked.

"But you saved me," she whispered. "It was *you*! You looked down from the wall and you smiled. You gave me courage and you told me what to do – even before we met by the river, it was you who helped me to escape."

The young man had now gone very white and his fingers, where she clasped them, felt suddenly cold.

"Who are you?" he asked her, his voice strained. "Where have you come from?"

She shook her head.

"I must not tell you, I cannot. They must never find me."

Now he took both her hands in his.

"You don't have to tell me, as I think I know – "

"How? How can you know?" she asked him and then she saw the look in his dark eyes and, though she did not understand how or why, she knew that he did know the truth about her and that in some way he was deeply upset by it.

There was a sudden blast of laughter and voices just behind them from inside the ballroom and the window next to them was pushed wide open.

"Here she is!"

The Contessa's ringing voice stabbed at Rosella's ears.

"Come, my English Rose – here is a fine English gentleman who insists that he must dance with you."

She seized Rosella's hand.

"Where is your mask?" she hissed, pulling it from where Rosella had tucked it into her belt. "What do you mean by taking it off?"

She then glared at the young man in the turban and pushed the mask roughly back onto Rosella's face.

And next she thrust her towards a portly gentleman whose large body amply filled the baggy pantaloons of his Harlequin costume.

"I say, Contessa, what a little beauty! Just look at those pretty curls!"

The man's words rang in Rosella's ears in a strange distorted way, as if she were hearing them from the other end of a long tunnel.

Harlequin grabbed her waist and pulled her onto the dance floor, the long nose of his white masked bobbing in front of her face.

She moved with him in slow circles, following his clumsy steps as if in a trance.

But she saw nothing except the dark eyes that had just been fixed on her face and the echo of his voice saying over and over, "*you don't have to tell me, as I think I know!*" drowned out the loud and foolish comments of Harlequin as he pulled her across the dance floor.

\*

Lyndon fled from the ballroom and then wandered through an endless maze of dark alleys without any idea of where he was heading.

His heart felt as if it had been split wide open and a torrent of painful emotions surged up inside him, so that he had to keep walking on and on.

He had just seen a vision of perfect beauty in the ballroom – a woman, tall and slender in a gorgeous silk gown and with golden hair streaming over her shoulders.

A woman lovelier than he had ever pictured, when he imagined all the beauties of Venice he might flirt with.

He had danced with her and she had flown across the ballroom with him as if they were twin souls.

And then she had torn the jewelled mask from her face and he had seen how young she was, how innocent and vulnerable.

He shivered as he recalled how she had struggled to tell him her story, how the tears had shone in her blue eyes and her voice had faltered as she described the man who had inherited her aunt's home.

She had mentioned no names, but it had to be his father. Lyndon had heard about the death of Beatrice, Lord Brockley's sister.

And he knew that his father would be taking over her home, New Hall.

But much worse than that, the disgusting Algernon Merriman, for surely it was he, must have been at New Hall as well and he had proposed to her and tried to force himself upon her.

At one moment Lyndon felt pity for the girl and at the next he was consumed with rage and horror at the very thought that Merriman's fat hands had touched her and that he may have even pressed his thick lips against her sweet mouth.

Perhaps the best thing he could do would be leap into the canal and let the dark waters close over his head.

But then he would drown the image of her beauty too and the vision of her lovely face that filled his mind.

And he would never see her again.

Lyndon walked and walked, until totally exhausted, he leaned up against the brick wall of an ancient house.

Up above him the sky was turning green as dawn approached and one large star glowed brightly.

At last his feelings were beginning to calm down and the only sensation that filled his heart was pain.

What hurt was not that she had become embroiled with his father and Algernon Merriman, but a growing fear that he might lose her.

'I love her,' he told himself and the words seemed to echo along the alley, bouncing off the walls and losing themselves in the water of the nearby canal.

He could not deceive so innocent and gentle a girl, use her for fun and harmless flirtation as he had planned. He could only love, adore and worship her.

He must be as honest and candid with her as she had been to him.

But what would she think of him, if she knew that he was Lord Brockley's son?

If indeed he spoke to her and told her who he was, she might recoil from him in horror and the sweet openness and trust she had shown his masked self on the balcony would turn to loathing and disgust.

No matter that he had repudiated his family, that he was deeply ashamed of them, she would see on his face the hated Brockley features and be repulsed by him.

Then it came to him exactly what he must do.

'I will write to her,' he decided, pressing his head against the wall. 'I will tell her everything. I will tell her who I am and that I love her and I will ask her, if she could bear to, to meet me when she has had time to think about it all.'

The sky was growing lighter every minute and he realised that he had been up all night.

He must hurry back to his room and compose the letter and then he would deliver it to the Palazzo himself.

*

When Rosella woke up, there were rays of bright sunlight shining through the slats of the shutters and onto her silk bedcover.

'I have overslept,' she reflected. 'It's very late.'

Her head was throbbing and her heart felt heavy.

She had no memory of going to bed last night, only of looking for the young man everywhere in the ballroom and on the balcony, but he was nowhere to be seen.

She could not erase from her mind the picture of his troubled eyes gazing at her through the velvet mask, as she told him her story.

And yet, what Heaven it had been to dance with him. Surely, now that they had found each other, he would come back to her.

Mimi tapped at the bedroom door and came in with a tray of tea and pastries.

"*Signorina*," she whispered, bending low over the bed. "You must get up! There is someone to see you. A gentleman. *Un Inglese!*"

An Englishman!

Joy flooded through Rosella's body and she felt her headache evaporating as she sat up.

He had come! He was waiting for her downstairs.

She would see him in just a few moments in the bright light of day without a mask, just himself right there in front of her.

"Come on, Rosella," the Contessa said, opening the door of her private salon, a little frown on her lined face.

"There is someone here who is very eager to speak with you."

Her heart in her mouth, Rosella then stepped into the salon.

And there, sprawled over one of the Contessa's best velvet chairs, was *Algernon Merriman*, a wide smile on his face.

"Well, my sweetheart!" he crowed. "At last I have found you. Your friend the Contessa was very surprised to hear that we are engaged. But she says there will be no problem arranging a marriage, as soon as may be."

He pulled himself out of the chair.

"I have always liked the idea of a honeymoon in Venice," he sighed, as he reached to embrace Rosella.

*

Lyndon sighed.

Much to his annoyance he had emerged from the maze of alleyways on the opposite side of the Grand Canal from the Palazzo and now he would have to go back on his tracks and find a bridge.

He stood for a moment, gazing up at the balcony where he and the beautiful girl had stood last night.

He did not even know her name, but that would soon change, if she read his letter and agreed to meet him.

Suddenly he heard raised voices and the shutters of one of the rooms above the ballroom burst open.

A grey bird with a red tail fluttered out and Lyndon saw it fly up into the sunshine and disappear.

"Pickle! No!" a girl's voice, torn with despair, rang out.

And then he saw her in the window, her fair hair catching the sunlight.

Lyndon waved to her and held up the letter with his heart pounding, but behind her a bulky figure loomed.

A man in a grey morning coat with a round face and an all-too-familiar pointed moustache.

Lyndon watched in horror as the man seized the girl in his arms and pressed her to him, burying his moustache in her golden curls as he kissed the top of her head over and over again.

Lyndon took his letter and tore it in two, before throwing it into the canal.

He waited a moment, hoping the pieces of paper would sink, but they bobbed on top of the water, moving away from him like two tiny boats.

He turned on his heel and ran back into the maze of alleys.

# CHAPTER TEN

"What is going on?"

The Contessa stormed into her salon.

"And where is *Signore Papagallo*?"

She then stared at the open window, her thin black eyebrows arched with rage.

"Did I not see him, just now, flying away over the rooftops?"

"If you are referring to that useless bird, he has just bitten my finger to the bone!" Algernon growled, clutching Rosella to him with one arm and waving the other hand in the air to show off his injury.

"It was my absolute pleasure to fling him out of the window!"

The Contessa gave him a black look, but she said no more on the subject, but instead she turned her fury onto Rosella.

"Why did you not tell me that you were *fidanzata*?" she shouted. "And that you have promised to marry this gentleman?"

"I did not promise anything," Rosella gasped.

She could hardly speak, as Algernon seemed to be doing his best to crush the breath from her body.

"Oh yes, you did!" he cried and then he whispered into Rosella's ear, "and if you had not been so foolish as to write to the gardener's boy, of all the ridiculous things, telling him that you were in Venice, you might have got away with breaking your promise – you wicked girl!"

"*Vergogna!*" shrilled the Contessa, stabbing at the floor with her walking stick. "Are you not very ashamed of yourself – that you allowed me to go to all the trouble of holding a *Ballo in Maschera* for you, when all the time you have a fiancé?"

Algernon clasped Rosella to him.

"Ah, Contessa, if you had not, I would never have found her again. I knew that she was in Venice – but not exactly where – and at your ball here last night, I thought I recognised her golden hair. And now, this morning, when I see her without the mask, of course, it's my sweetheart!"

He lavished more kisses on top of Rosella's head, which was all he could reach, as she kept her face turned down away from him.

"Please do stop! I will never marry you," Rosella screamed out in utter despair. "I cannot!"

The Contessa gave a squeal of anger and attacked Algernon with her stick, driving him away from Rosella.

For a blissful moment, Rosella's heart swelled with the hope that the Contessa was trying to protect her, but then the old woman seized a handful of Rosella's hair and pulled it painfully.

"What are you saying, girl?" she hissed. "This man tells me you promised to marry him and now you would go back on your word. I will not have such behaviour under my roof. Out of my house! Now!"

She gave Rosella's hair another fierce tug, dragging her towards the door.

"What are you doing, Contessa?" Algernon cried, staring at her in alarm and holding his bitten finger high in the air so that drops of blood ran down into his cuff.

"Silence!" the Contessa yelled. "What kind of man are you that you let your promised wife run away from you so easily? You must be a fool!"

"Well – charming!" Algernon stuttered. "You quite clearly have no better manners than that disgusting parrot!"

If Rosella had not been in such pain from her pulled hair and in such fear as to what might happen next, she might have laughed at him because he was a most pathetic and comical sight.

The Contessa shoved Rosella towards the staircase.

"Out of my house!" she demanded her voice icy cold. "Don't even think of coming back."

"But my things – " Rosella began.

"Out!" the Contessa shouted.

It was no use, Rosella would have to leave – right away – without even collecting her carpet bag.

She longed to run to a window and look down onto the opposite bank of the Canal, for she was sure that, just a moment ago, she had glimpsed a familiar figure there, clad in a long dark cloak and a wide hat.

But she did not dare to hesitate any longer and she ran down the stairs and found her way to the side door of the Palazzo.

The statue of the man in the turban was still there, but today his smile seemed only to mock and the waters of the Grand Canal that she had once found so cool and fresh seemed stagnant and noxious.

Rosella stood, tears stinging her eyes, not knowing what she should do and then she heard a low whistle above her head.

Mimi was leaning out of a window with the carpet bag in her hand. As Rosella looked up, she let go of it, so that it fell down into her arms.

Then Mimi held her finger to her lips and pointed to further down the Canal.

The carved prow of Giovanni's large gondola was inching silently through the water towards Rosella.

As he drew nearer, Giovanni raised his finger to his lips in the same gesture that Mimi had just used.

"Quick, *Signorina*," he whispered, "jump!"

As the gondola slid past her, Rosella leapt from the steps of the Palazzo and landed on the velvet cushions.

The slender craft swayed in the water, but such was Giovanni's skill that he held it steady and then lifted his oar to push it swiftly and soundlessly forward.

Something small and white then caught Rosella's eye floating past her in the water of the Grand Canal. She must have dropped her handkerchief as she jumped.

She reached down to catch it.

But it was not her white silk handkerchief. It was a piece of thick writing paper that had been torn in half.

The two halves were stuck together, one of top of the other, so that they floated on the surface of the canal like a little raft.

Words were written on the writing paper in a bold, masculine hand in blue ink, words that were fast becoming illegible from the water.

Rosella prised the two damp pieces of paper apart and peered at the writing.

*"My dearest love, for that is what you are.*

*There has never been another, nor will there ever be –*

So many of the words were blurred and smudged by the water that it was hard to read, but it seemed to be a love letter.

*I could not bear to leave – your words tore me apart – still I love you – but you must know that I too have a past –*

Even while she gazed at them, the sentences were melting into a pool of watery blue ink.

*My father – utterly thoughtless and without scruple – I cannot –*

What could it mean? The very last words at the bottom of one of the pieces of paper, gave her heart a jolt that almost caused her to faint.

*Please, please – I must see you again – if you can only forgive my name, which must be utterly hateful to you and understand – that I am most truly – and forever,*

*yours –*

*Lord Lyndon Brockley."*

Lord Lyndon *Brockley*? Were these words penned by a relation of the hateful Lord Brockley? By his *son*, even!

And was it possible that this letter was intended for her? She stared at the words and read them over and over, until at last she understood. It was Lord Lyndon Brockley she had danced with last night.

Her mind whirled round with a thousand confusing and conflicting emotions. She had given away her secret to the son of the very man who had threatened her happiness!

Yet she could not forget how they had seemed like two halves of the same being, as they both flew across the ballroom together.

And did he not say in this letter something about his father being without scruple and thoughtless?

She stared at the pieces of paper once again, but the words had vanished, melting into a sea of indistinguishable blue marks.

"*Signorina*," Giovanni was calling her name softly. "Don't be sad, *Signorina*. You will be safe. I take you to Mamma and you will see, all will be good!"

But Rosella did not care too much where he was taking her.

Everything was ruined and broken.

The man who said he loved her was the son of her enemy and her benefactor, the Contessa, had cast her out.

Even her beloved parrot, the last link with the old kind world she once knew was lost forever in this City that now seemed alien and hostile to her.

But worst of all was the realisation that her vision of the ballroom and the illusion of the young man in the painting had been false and dangerous mirages that had led her astray.

Giovanni brought the gondola to a halt at the edge of the City. He leapt onto the shore and tapped Rosella on the shoulder.

"*Signorina*, come. My friend take you onwards. It is long way and I must go back or the Contessa will – "

He mimed drawing a sharp knife across his throat.

Rosella stumbled to her feet. Next to the gondola was an old rowing boat filled with sacks with an old man at the helm.

She clambered aboard and sat down on one of the sacks, brushing aside the dry onions and withered carrots that lay there.

The old man grunted and pulled on the oars with his wiry arms and the boat moved slowly out into the wide waters of the Lagoon.

Rosella blinked at the glare of the bright sunshine on the pearly water, as the little boat passed by the familiar island of Murano and made its way toward the hazy blue horizon.

Giovanni was right.

They had a long way to travel.

Someone was tapping at Lyndon's window, calling to him in an odd croaky voice,

"*Hello! Hello!*"

He sat up in his bed and rubbed his eyes. Who the hell was trying to wake him up?

It was very dark in the room as Lyndon had kept the shutters closed against the bright summer sun and also against the smell of the stagnant canal water that drifted up in the heat.

How could he ever have thought that Venice was a beautiful place?

It was August now, several weeks since the night of the *Ballo in Maschera* and the sun beat down relentlessly over the City.

Even at night it was too hot and the brick walls of the buildings seemed to give back into the darkness all the heat of the sunshine they had absorbed through the day.

Everything that had once seemed to him mysterious and exciting – the dark alleyways, the deep green water of the canals – now seemed sinister and unpleasant.

"*Hello! Hello!*"

The strange cry came again and the shutter rattled.

Lyndon then reluctantly staggered out of bed. He had spent long enough hiding in this room, he thought, as he padded across in his bare feet to open the window.

It was time to move on. Perhaps to somewhere like Switzerland, to the clean bright mountains.

He was still half asleep, so it was not until he was about to pull open the shutters that he remembered that his room was on the fourth floor of the building.

His heart skipped a beat.

Was he going quite mad after so long cooped up in this place? Or had some lunatic climbed all the way up the side of the house to pester him?

Lyndon peered through one of the narrow slits in the wooden shutters and a round eye with a black pupil and a pale gold rim stared back at him.

This was no human eye. It seemed to belong to some kind of little imp, some supernatural manifestation of this uncanny City.

Lyndon was about to run out of his room and rush down the stairs to shout for Fabio, who lived below him, when the imp spoke again.

"*Good Morning!*" it piped up in a perfect English accent.

Lyndon paused and opened the shutter a crack.

There, sitting on the windowsill was the grey parrot that he had first met in London by the River Thames.

It had to be the same one! For had he not seen a grey bird with a bright red tail, flying away from the *Ca'degli Angeli* on that terrible morning when he had tried to deliver his letter to the girl of his dreams –

Lyndon brushed the memory of that awful moment out of his mind. There was nothing to do but put it all behind him.

No doubt she was happily in the arms of Algernon Merriman by now. Perhaps they were even married. He must not think about her again.

Rosella. That was her name. He knew it now as all of Venice had been talking of her disappearance after the ball.

He shook his head to banish the painful thoughts.

But what should he do with this bird?

It was looking rather bedraggled and one of its tail feathers was broken and bent sideways.

He opened the window and then the parrot climbed clumsily in. It flew across the room and sat on the back of the chair by his desk.

"*Is it time for tea?*" the bird asked him in a polite tone and then added, "*may I have a nut?*"

Lyndon found himself smiling for the first time since the morning after the ball.

"I shall have some sent up for us, if you like," he joked. "English tea and a plate of walnuts, what do you say?"

"*Good afternoon, Pickle!*" the bird replied and flew across to sit on his shoulder.

Now Lyndon was laughing.

Pickle! That was the bird's name, he remembered.

He reached up to stroke the bird's head.

"So, Pickle, she has deserted you too. But we shall not think about her any more, shall we? We must forget her and get on with our lives. What do you say to that?"

"*You're a very naughty boy!*" Pickle replied, but he seemed to like Lyndon, as he nibbled gently on his finger and seemed happy to stay sitting on his shoulder.

*

Rosella and Mimi sat quietly in the shade of a vine, shelling peas into a large china bowl.

The garden where they sat was heavenly, Rosella thought. It was so luscious and so abundant with the green leaves of the vine hanging over their head and everywhere she looked vegetables were growing – pumpkins, tomatoes and cucumbers – everything bursting with life and energy.

Through the leaves she could see the sun shining on the wide waters of the Lagoon.

"You and Giovanni were very lucky to grow up here," she said to Mimi. "It's like Paradise."

Mimi nodded.

Just after the Contessa had thrown Rosella out, the maid had left her position at the Ca' degli Angeli and come home to this green island on the far side of the Lagoon, where lush kitchen gardens supplied the markets of Venice with produce.

"It's my home," she replied. "I am always happy here with Mamma."

"It is so kind of your family to take me in," Rosella said, hurriedly opening a few more pea pods, as Giovanni was due to visit them and Mamma was cooking a risotto with peas and artichokes.

She had already called out from the kitchen in the house several times for the girls to hurry up.

Mimi shrugged in her expressive Italian way.

"It was nothing. You are angel, Mamma says. And for me, you are *mia sorella* – my sister! I have always wanted a sister."

"I wish that you had not had to lose your job – "

"I did not," Mimi interrupted her. "I left! I did not want to stay and work for the Contessa anymore, after she was so unkind to you."

"But – "

"*Signorina*, you must not speak of this again. If I want to work, there are many families in Venice who will take me. But I am so happy here – we have everything we need."

Rosella looked at the garden, at all its richness and beauty glowing in the golden sunshine.

It was strange to think that she had been here now for almost a month.

Mimi was so right. There was everything here that anyone might ever need, but her heart still felt empty and cold and, in spite of the loving and affectionate family that surrounded her, she felt lonely and abandoned.

If only –

But she must not think of the young man she had danced with. He was a mirage, an illusion, something she had dreamt up in her longing to be loved and cared for.

He might have thought he cared for her, perhaps, for a moment or two, but his love had not lasted.

Almost as soon as he had written the love letter to her, he had torn it in half.

His feelings for her had melted and vanished, just as the words he had put on the paper had disappeared into a blue smudge.

He was Lord Brockley's son and that was the only thing that mattered. He was the son of a man she detested and hated.

"*Buon giorno.*"

A man's voice called. Giovanni was coming up the path into the garden.

His black eyes glowed when he saw Rosella sitting with his sister.

He greeted Mimi and then he took Rosella's hand in his broad strong grip and raised it to his lips.

'I think that he is beginning to care a little for me,' she thought. 'And I should be grateful as I must think how I am to survive when all of Aunt Beatrice's sovereigns are gone.'

But her heart did not stir at Giovanni's touch and her eyes could not meet his.

*

Lyndon peered over the backs of the women who were thronging around the colourful displays of fruit and vegetables in the market.

"We are out of luck, old chap," he sighed to Pickle, who was gripping tightly onto his shoulder. "It's not the time of year for nuts yet."

The bird seemed to have grown fond of Lyndon and seemed quite happy to continue sitting on his shoulder.

It was certainly far better to bring him out than to leave him behind on his own, when he would scream and scream and disturb the whole building.

"What would you think of those cherries, eh? Or perhaps a peach?"

Lyndon bent over a colourful display of fruit.

Suddenly Pickle gave a squawk, flapped his wings and was gone, flying over the market stalls.

"Hey, come back," Lyndon called out.

But the bird had not gone far.

He had landed on the blue hood of a market girl, who was helping another young woman to unload several baskets of bright red tomatoes onto a stall.

Lyndon pushed his way through the excited crowd, who were pointing and laughing.

"Bad bird! Come back here!" he shouted.

Pickle did not budge. The girl did not seem afraid at having such a large bird landing on her head and she was reaching up to pet him.

"I'm sorry," Lyndon began and then his heart stood still, as her blue eyes looked at him and he saw the gold hair escaping from under her hood.

"Thank God! It's you!" he exclaimed.

She turned away, as if she was afraid of him.

"Please, please we must talk – " Lyndon now found himself gabbling, the words tumbling over each other,

"I – have thought of you every moment – I cannot lose you again."

He fell onto his knees among all the debris of the marketplace and caught her hand, holding it to his lips.

A wave of joy broke over his body as she turned back to him and he felt her fingers touch his hair.

Rosella's heart soared at the same time.

Her dream man from the painting at New Hall had appeared once again in her life and this time she absolutely knew that he would stay with her for ever.

It was her destiny, and his, written in the stars thousands of years ago.

*

Summer was almost over in Venice and a cold wind was blowing off the Adriatic, as Rosella and Lyndon stood on the wide golden sands of the Lido, waiting for the boat that was to come and carry them away to Greece.

"Where is Giovanni, do you think?" Rosella asked. "He said he would come before dark."

A tremor of fear stirred in her heart, as she knew that the handsome gondolier had been more than a little in love with her.

It must have been hard for him to see her over the last few weeks always with Lyndon.

But he had promised to help them. He was a good man, he would not let them down surely.

"He will come, he gave us his word."

Lyndon drew her nearer to him, holding her against the warmth of his body.

"Soon we will be far away from prying eyes and it will be just the two of us and then we will be married," he sighed.

She closed her eyes, feeling the complete bliss of his nearness.

"When I think of all the times that I almost flung myself into the Grand Canal, just like Lord Osborne did," he was saying.

Rosella shivered, for the thought that he might have ended his life, destroying for ever the incredible happiness they both now felt, was unbearable.

"Now that I have found you again, I am so utterly happy," he continued and pressed his lips to her forehead.

She felt her happiness bloom inside her, like a full-blown, sweet-scented rose.

"The days I have spent with you in that garden on the island have made me want to live forever," Lyndon said and she felt the passion in his voice vibrating through her body.

"To be with you always, Rosella. I did not know that life – that love, could be like this."

Now his lips found hers and Rosella felt her soul fly to join with his, as her body lay against his warmth and strength.

His kisses then took her into the sky and she was touching the stars and the moon all at the same time, as he became more passionate and demanding.

"But, my love, we will have so little," he said after a moment.

"I would love you if you had nothing," she replied at once, hating to see the look of doubt that shadowed his eyes.

"And Pickle – you told me once that you would never part with him."

Rosella laughed.

"He is in parrot Heaven!" she said. "Mimi and her Mamma adore him. He has all the fruit and vegetables he can eat and a storeroom full of nuts! It would be cruel of me to take him away."

Lyndon smiled.

"I shall miss that bird," he sighed, "but I think you are right."

Her reassurance had made him happy again and the brightness in his face reminded her of the painting in her bedroom at New Hall.

She knew now that it was a portrait of his ancestor, Lord Osborne. It had been painted in Venice and sent home to England after Osborne's death.

Rosella understood too that her strange visions had not deceived her, as they had brought her to his moment and to the love that was the centre and the whole purpose of her life.

Perhaps the spirit of Lord Osborne, who had met such a sad end, had conspired to bring her here to ensure a happy ending for her and Lyndon.

Now he gripped her arm.

"Look, Rosella!"

A tall ship had appeared just offshore and sailors were rushing to bring down the full sails so that she might come to a standstill.

"It's *La Maschera*, Lyndon gasped. "I saw her in Limehouse. The Contessa's ship."

"We must run!" Rosella cried, her heart pounding.

But there was nowhere to hide on the wide empty beach of the Lido.

Now she could hear, faintly on the wind, someone calling her name.

"It's Giovanni," Rosella said, her heart sinking, as she saw the gondolier climbing over the side of the ship and leaping into a rowing boat.

"He – must have told the Contessa."

How could it be that in one moment her happiness could turn to such black despair?

Lyndon gripped her cold fingers tightly.

"Wait, my love," he urged. "Giovanni is all alone, he cannot force us to go with him."

Rosella shivered at the thought of the gondolier's strong hands and brawny arms, so powerful from years of plying the oar of the gondola.

What would happen if it came to a fight?

But Lyndon was without fear.

"Be brave, my darling," he said. "I will not let you come to harm."

The rowing boat drove into the sandy edge of the beach and Giovanni leapt out.

He ran towards them, a large white envelope in his hand.

"Giovanni – what are you doing?" Rosella began. "You promised you would help us."

He held out the envelope.

"A letter came for you, *Signorina*."

Puzzled, Rosella took the envelope from him.

It was indeed addressed to her and in large uneven letters, as if a child had written it. She would read it when they were safely on their way to Greece.

"Giovanni, we must leave tonight – you said you would find a boat for us."

The gondolier bowed his head.

"*Signorina*, I have come from the Contessa. Her mood has been so dark, so bitter, since you left. When the letter came and she saw your name, she wept, *Signorina*. She cried out that she could not forgive herself for sending you away. And I told her – "

"Oh, Giovanni – "

Rosella felt tears of disappointment spring into her eyes. The gondolier had betrayed her just as she suspected.

"Wait, *Signorina*. Listen! I told her you were safe and happy and that you were with your love."

Giovanni glanced over at Lyndon and there was a brief moment of regret in his black eyes, but he quickly continued,

"I told her that you wished to marry him and to go somewhere far away from Italy, from England, from the people that might know you."

"How could you?" Lyndon cried.

"*Signore*, I did what I thought was right and the Contessa told me, 'if they wish to go, Giovanni, then let my ship carry them wherever they wish to go and I will ask no questions. But if they will come back to the *Ca' degli Angeli*, I would welcome them with my open heart.' She is a good woman, *Signore*."

Lyndon shook his head, bemused.

"Rosella, what do you make of it?"

"I – don't know – I can't think," Rosella said, torn between a great longing to see the Contessa again and an even greater desire to leave everything behind and set sail at once for Greece with Lyndon.

Giovanni was clearly waiting for their answer, but she simply did not know what to do.

"What about your letter?" Lyndon said suddenly.

He took it from her.

"Who has written to you?"

"I don't know," Rosella replied. "I don't suppose it matters now. Read it, if you want to."

Her need to be gone and to escape was growing stronger, as she looked at the graceful ship that stood just off the shore.

Lyndon then slit open the envelope and, as his eyes skimmed the contents, he turned very pale.

"What is it?"

"My darling Rosella, I think we will not be going to Greece, after all."

"But – why not?"

Lyndon reached to take her hand.

He seemed to have grown taller suddenly and a new strength had come into his face.

"Your letter is from someone called Thomas," he said. "Your gardener's boy you told me about."

"Thomas?"

Rosella remembered the brown-haired lad who had helped her and then had inadvertently led Mr. Merriman to find her in Venice.

"There are few words – but he says he is sorry that the Head Gardener opened your letter and gave it to his Lordship."

"That is all in the past now –" Rosella began, but Lyndon had not finished.

"And he says that my father, Carlton Brockley is dead. What is this – I cannot quite – "

Lyndon frowned as he tried to decipher Thomas's handwriting.

Rosella suddenly realised how cold she was in the wind that blew off the sea.

"Ah! He became ill at dinner one night and died suddenly."

Lyndon turned to Rosella, his expression grave, yet his eyes shining with a new clear light.

"We shall not be going to Greece, my darling. I am taking you home."

"What do you mean?"

"I am his only son. New Hall is mine now. *I can take you home.*"

Rosella was speechless, as the joy that filled her heart was pulling it up and up like a kite into the patch of blue sky that was opening up in the clouds above them and she cried,

"Look, Lyndon. The sun is coming out!"

"Yes. We shall have a fair voyage home."

He caught her to his breast and she closed her eyes, surrendering to the heavenly bliss of being in his arms once more.

"But shall we go and see the Contessa first?" she whispered after a moment.

"Of course," he answered. "And before we leave we must give our thanks to Venice – *La Serenissima* – the serene and lovely City that brought us together."

"I shall never forget her," Rosella sighed, "she will always have a special place in our hearts."

Lyndon then caught her up in his arms in the bright sunshine and carried her to the rowing boat to begin their joyful journey home to their new life together.